DRAWN TO THE PAST

EVELYN & LEO ROMANTIC SUSPENSE SERIES
BOOK THREE

KAT SHEHATA

ANGEL BEA PUBLISHING

For Ash and JoJo

PROLOGUE

*S*loane Matthews

No one will miss me if I slip away for an hour.

All my friends were at the bonfire tonight for the annual Halloween bash, and I was dressed up in my Little Red Riding Hood costume for the occasion.

I lived for the spooky season and embraced the pumpkin-spiced lattes, ghostly goodies, witchy black cats, and all the fall fetishes celebrated this time of year.

The perfect excuse to cosplay with my fairytale-obsessed boyfriend.

He wanted to keep our relationship a secret, so we made plans to meet in a remote location not far from the party. I took a few sips of warm beer from my plastic cup to appear social, but butterflies of excitement fluttered in my stomach in anticipation of seeing him—Professor Bradford.

"Hey, Sloane," my roommate Lindsey hollered from the other side of the fire. "Cute costume!"

I twirled around in my red cloak and thanked her with a thumbs-up and a smile.

While my friends were rocking out to "Monster Mash," snuggling to keep warm next to the bonfire, and swapping horror stories about the fall semester, my thoughts kept circling back to my sexy and brilliant literature professor—the man I was madly in love with.

I made my rounds and chatted with my friends before heading to the nature path that would lead me to Mr. Nolan Bradford—the tenured professor. The crisp fall leaves crunched under my patent black shoes as I strolled through the woods to our secret meeting spot.

I smiled at the memory of our first meeting. We had an appointment to go over a critical essay on Romeo and Juliet that I'd bombed, and from the moment I walked into his office and sat on the edge of his desk, I knew by the way he focused all his attention on me that the attraction was mutual.

His intelligent brown eyes lit up when I complimented him on his whimsical socks. I noticed everything about my handsome professor, including the alligator design peeking out from under the hem of his dress pants.

"I love golf. My wife got these for me after a trip to Florida last summer."

So, the only bad thing about my boyfriend—he was married.

Once I trekked down the path and the bonfire was out of sight, I used the flashlight on my phone to guide me to our secret location. Nolan wanted to meet me on a deserted back road where no one from the party would find out about our affair.

As the music from the party and the collective buzz of people talking died down, I felt nervous about being alone in the middle of the woods on the outskirts of the city. I was, after all, from a small town where we never worried about locking our doors in the evening.

Chicago, however, was a dangerous place to roam around alone at night. I worried I might cross paths with a meth head or a psycho maniac just waiting for a dumbass freshman to trek through the freaking wilderness by herself to hook up with her married boyfriend.

But he won't be married for much longer.

Nolan and I were in love—no more secrets and lies. I was tired of sharing with another woman and wanted him all to myself. A few nights ago, after we made love in his car, I gave Nolan an ultimatum—her or me.

Tonight, I would find out his answer.

I gave him my virginity, my love, all my attention and adoration, but in the past, he'd refused to leave his wife, Cora. Nolan said he'd tried to divorce her for years, but their marriage was complicated.

I was almost at the end of the trail when I spotted Nolan's car on the side of the road. I knew it was him because I could see the fuzzy dice dangling from the rearview mirror.

I knew that Nolan would make up his mind—he'd choose me.

I smoothed my hair back, applied a fresh layer of cherry-flavored Chapstick to my lips, and inhaled a deep breath to calm the butterflies.

From that night on, I could tell the world that I, Sloane Matthews, was Professor Nolan Bradford's girlfriend. I would take him back to my hometown to meet my family over Thanksgiving break and introduce him to all my friends.

All the boys who never looked at me twice in high school would regret it when they saw me snuggled in the arms of my brilliant and handsome professor. And the prissy girls who treated me like a nobody would see—

Snap! Snap! Snap!

There was a shuffling sound in the woods a few feet away from the path. I used the light on my phone to search for signs of life.

"Nolan?"

I held my breath and listened for a reply.

Nothing.

Maybe it was a squirrel or a nocturnal animal scurrying around in the woods. I stayed on the path and aimed the light on the trail as I walked, careful not to trip over the slick rocks along the way.

I stopped when I noticed something shiny on the trail ahead. *Oh, my God.* I cracked up when I spotted a handful of condoms glistening like golden foil breadcrumbs leading me to our rendezvous point. It was the same brand Nolan used, so I knew it was him playing a game.

"Hilarious, Nolan. You can come out now. I'm getting a little spooked out here." I waited a moment, but he never responded. "Nolan?"

No response.

I kept walking and came across a pair of lacy black panties—they were mine. Nolan had removed them with his teeth the last time we'd made love. The professor had his share of kinks and fetishes and loved to explore the Dom side of his otherwise meek personality.

He liked to play rough and seduced me with a combination of pleasure and pain. I wanted to please him, but I was more into cuddling in a soft bed with pillows over bondage and spanking.

As I continued down the trail, I spotted a black carnation on the path, along with a photograph attached to the stem with a red ribbon. The picture was of Nolan and me having sex in his car.

What the hell? We were alone then, which meant Nolan

had planted a camera in his Volvo and had taken pictures without my consent. Maybe this was his strange way of apologizing to me.

Nolan and I had a lovers' quarrel on the night I'd given him the ultimatum. I was tired of sneaking around and wanted our relationship to go public, so I told Nolan he had to make a choice. If he was only interested in smutty sex, then I was out.

We argued about it, but I stood my ground. I hoped a few days apart would smooth things over. The thing that bothered me, though, was that right after our fight, someone sent a weird package to me.

It had about twenty photos of me at various locations on campus. A picture of me at the library, one at the dining hall, and another of me hanging out with friends in the common area.

Inside the package, there was also a receipt from a restaurant I had tossed in the garbage, a ticket stub from a football game I had attended, and a scrunchy I had misplaced after Nolan and I hooked up in his office after hours.

It didn't come with a note or anything, so I figured someone was playing a prank on me, but now that I found this random stuff here, in the woods where Nolan had said to meet him, I wondered if this was Nolan's kinky way of apologizing to me after our fight.

Where are you, Nolan?

I checked my phone for a message from him.

Nothing.

Nolan probably had his phone off. He was like that. The geeky guy who preferred to live in the moment and absorb his surroundings over clicking and scrolling mindlessly on his phone.

Snap! Snap! Snap!

Footsteps pounded toward me.

"Who's there?" I searched the woods to see who was charging toward me, but I became disoriented in the darkness. Instead of waiting for someone to ambush me, I hoofed it toward Nolan's car.

As I fled, I tripped over a branch and landed hard on my knee, ripping my white tights. I shined the light on my injury and felt nauseous when I saw a deep gash and blood oozing down my leg.

Mud and bits of leaves stuck to my skin, and I worried it would get infected with all that dirt caked in the wound. I could go to the campus clinic later. My bigger problem was limping out of the woods and reaching Nolan's car.

Pull yourself together, Sloane. This place was crawling with woodland creatures. The noise came from a squirrel or an opossum or a raccoon—

"Wither away so early, Little Red Riding Hood?" A voice called through the darkness.

I was frightened at first, but sighed in relief, knowing my boyfriend was the only nerd in the woods quoting the Brothers Grimm tonight. "Nolan, where are you? I need your help. I tripped over a branch. I'm bleeding."

I aimed my phone at the sound of his voice. "Honey? Is that you?" I shined the light into the darkness. Someone was there, standing in the woods, wearing a wolf mask. As I stared at the figure, neither one of us moved.

It had to be Nolan dressed as my counterpart, the Big Bad Wolf, but why then did I feel a deep sense of dread?

This felt wrong. I knew I made a mistake and needed to get back to the party. Slowly, I backed away, but as I retreated, the wolf pursued me.

I quickened my pace, but my leg was stiff and sore from the injury, and I couldn't break into a run. As I limped down the path, footsteps pounded behind me on the trail.

"Get away from me! Help!"

Wham!

A heavy body slammed into me with the force of a truck and knocked me off my feet. When my head hit the ground, the force of the blow nearly knocked me unconscious.

As I lay there, stunned, my attacker grabbed my ankles and dragged me through the woods off the beaten path. My Little Red Riding Hood costume rode up my back, and my bare skin scraped against the rocks and leaves and sticks that covered the earth.

I struggled against my attacker, but I was disoriented from my head injury and couldn't find the strength to free myself. I cried out for my friends, hoping someone could hear me back at the bonfire, but in the recesses of my mind, I knew I had strayed too far from the path.

Under the moonlit sky, I stared in horror as light reflected off the blade of an axe. Overcome with fear, I clawed at the dirt and kicked to slow my attacker down, but I was too weak from my injury to struggle free from my captor.

"Who are you? What do you want from me?"

My attacker answered my question by sliding off the mask.

Oh, God. No, no, no... A rush of fear and anger overcame me when I knew beyond doubt the identity of my attacker.

The wolf raised the axe above my head.

As the blade came down, I cursed my killer's name and vowed that my spirit would not leave this earth until I had my revenge.

SURPRISES—EVELYN

ne year later.

Leo snuggled me from behind and held me in his strong embrace as we stood in line at the coffee shop. His hand rested on my hip, then slid down my thigh. "You look gorgeous today, Evelyn," he whispered in my ear, then trailed kisses down my neck.

I bumped my backside against him to acknowledge his compliment. The physical attraction and adoration between us never dulled, and I couldn't imagine my life without him.

The coffee shop buzzed with activity as the morning rush crowded the counter to get a look at the day's special bakery treats. Leo and I were next in line, and I was suffering from a bad case of order anxiety. The seasonal selections of warm apple tarts, pumpkin fritters, and cinnamon-swirled goodies all screamed my name.

"What should I get, babe? Everything looks good."

"Get something with frosting so I can lick it off your body," Leo whispered.

My cheeks warmed with embarrassment. I lifted my scarf to hide my face as I cracked up at Leo's naughty joke. There was something different about Leo today. All of his attention was on me. His energy was electric. I was so happy Leo was in such a frisky and loving mood—but this was even a lot for him.

My serious, all-business boyfriend had been in a fun and flirty mood since we opened our eyes this morning. He usually saved his affectionate ways for when we were alone, but this morning, Leo was more playful in public than usual.

When it was our turn to order, Leo got a healthy protein drink, and I chose a vanilla cappuccino. "And we'll take two of your special cinnamon rolls to go. Can you choose the ones with the most icing for me?"

Leo pinched my backside to congratulate me on my choice.

As we enjoyed our drinks at our favorite corner table, I absorbed the energy of the festive fall vibe. It was officially sweater weather, and my fellow Chicagoans donned their rusty browns, golden yellows, and alpine green warm and fuzzy fashions.

Leo never changed his style for the seasons and stayed true to his off-duty style of dark jeans, form-fitting t-shirts, and now that the weather had turned chilly, a black leather jacket. My sexy boyfriend was the hottest cop in the city, and his dark style paired perfectly with his don't fuck with me vibe.

As I admired Leo's big, muscular body from across the table, he busted me checking him out. I shifted my gaze to the bakery box, lifted the lid, and inhaled the deliciously sweet scent of cinnamon and vanilla. "Heavenly."

While Leo smiled at my suggestive remark, his cell

vibrated on the table. He ignored it. It was out of character for Leo not to answer his phone, but he was off duty and had promised to give me all his attention today.

We had both taken off work and spending time together with no distractions was my idea of heaven. Even so, I was a creature of habit and wanted to sketch while I sipped my coffee. Drawing was like breathing, and my artistic soul didn't have an off switch.

I PULLED my art supplies out of my bag and placed the tip of my graphite pencil on a clean sheet of paper. I glanced around the room in search of an interesting subject for my sketch.

Worker bees getting their morning buzz on, business pros barking into their phones, teenagers snapping selfies with their precious pumpkin spice lattes…

"No drawing this morning." Leo plucked the pencil out of my grasp. "I've got an entire day with you, and I don't want any surprises—at least not that kind." He aimed his finger at the blank page.

"Whatever you say, Detective." I laughed as I followed his order and closed my sketchbook. Leo and I were not a typical couple. His request for a peaceful day was not because he was a control freak—it was more like an act of self-preservation.

Leo was a homicide detective. I was a medium who communicated with restless spirits through my art. My drawings of the dead had nearly gotten us both killed. Asking for a ghost-free day was not an unreasonable demand in our relationship.

"Do we have plans today, or are we going to wing it?" I asked.

Leo reached across the table and held my hand. "Do you trust me, Evelyn?"

His smoldering brown eyes held my attention as I contemplated my response. His vibe pulsed with an energy of excitement, and I didn't know what he was up to, but my sixth sense alerted me that something monumental was about to happen.

"I trust you with my life, babe."

His phone buzzed again, this time with an incoming call. His gaze never drifted from mine, but I knew the dedicated detective was dying to check his messages.

Since the moment Leo and I had met, our lives had bounced from one life-altering situation to another. I had narrowly escaped the clutches of a serial killer, and Leo had survived a mob hit.

Our lives would never be dull, but I hoped our next adventure would lead us down a less dangerous path. As a Chicago P.D. homicide detective, Leo's job was demanding. The messages might be from his partner, an informant, a witness, his team updating him on an ongoing investigation…

"Glad to hear that," Leo said. "Because today is all about—"

His cell buzzed for the umpteenth time. Someone really needed to reach him.

"Answer it," I said.

"I promised you my full attention today. Parker can handle whatever it is."

"Answer it, Detective. We have the entire day together."

"That's one of the many reasons why I love you, Evelyn." He snatched his phone and tapped the screen. "Detective Ricci."

Leo listened to the caller and pulled out his notepad to jot something down. "Where are you?" Leo's eyes sharpened. "You want to meet now?"

Day off or not, the information from the caller was important enough for him to want to meet the caller in person. I never wanted to hinder Leo's career or appear unsupportive, so I tapped my pointy fingernail on the table to get Leo's attention. "Go," I whispered.

Leo's gaze shot to mine. "Are you sure?"

"Positive."

"I'll be there in ten minutes," Leo said to the caller.

Before he left, he gave me a quick smooch on the lips, promised to be home in an hour, and told me he loved me. As he raced out the door, he called his partner. "Hey, we might have a break in the Sloane Matthews case. Meet me at…"

As Leo left the coffee shop and disappeared into a crowd of commuters, I nearly stood up and called him back to me. I had the unsettling sensation that something was wrong.

But then, he was a homicide detective. Danger was the nature of the job, and I had to live with that realization every day of our lives.

DREAD—EVELYN

We had the pleasure of dog-sitting a retired police K9 for a couple of days. To pass the time, I brought Duke to the dog park to get some exercise while I waited for Leo to finish up with work.

Leo's good friend and fellow officer had gone on her honeymoon and asked us to take care of Duke while she was out of town. We loved dogs and were happy to care for the sweet boy.

"Want to play ball, Duke?" I tossed a tennis ball as far as I could manage. "Search?"

The energetic yellow lab chased the ball, then obediently returned and dropped it at my feet. I praised the hard-working search and rescue officer and scratched him behind the ears.

I lifted the saliva-soaked tennis ball and held it up to get his attention. "Want me to throw it again?"

The dog cocked his head and zeroed in on the toy. Duke had only been staying with us for a few days, but I had already fallen in love with this loyal and loving big boy.

"Search!" I tossed the ball the length of the dog park and

smiled as Duke played his favorite game. During his career, he had received awards and praise for his service to our community.

Duke had been credited with tracking down missing persons, locating suspects on the run, and recovering remains at crime scenes. While I was grateful to have Duke for a short time, I hoped I could convince Leo to adopt a dog of our own someday.

Thinking of Leo, it surprised me he hadn't called yet. He said he'd be home in an hour, but he had been gone for twice as long. I checked my phone to see if I had any messages.

Nothing.

No reply to my text about going to the dog park, and no update on when he might return home. Not receiving an immediate response was normal, considering his line of work.

Don't worry, Evelyn. Leo will call soon.

But today was one of the rare occasions Leo had scheduled off work. My sexy boyfriend told me to clear my calendar for the entire day. His energy was off the charts, and I sensed he was planning something special.

Is it a sexy surprise?

The kind of activity that would keep us in bed all day? Thinking of spending the day under the sheets with my gorgeous, muscular boyfriend sent warm ripples of pleasure to my core.

Or is the surprise a thing?

I wondered if Leo was going to surprise me with a thoughtful gift and an evening at one of our favorite restaurants. We hadn't had a date night in a while, and I loved the idea of sharing a bottle of wine and spending quality time together without the distractions of our busy careers.

Please call me, Leo. Tell me everything is alright.

Although I tried to convince myself that everything was

fine, I had an unsettled feeling in my gut that something horrible had happened. When we first became a couple, I learned to train my thoughts and focus on the positive side of dating a detective.

Leo was brave and protective. Living with a highly trained and respected law enforcement officer gave me comfort—

Duke started barking to get my attention.

I glanced up to see what was troubling him. From where I was standing, I could see his bright yellow tennis ball under the bushes. The dog had reverted to working dog mode and was alerting me—his handler—that he had located his target and required help to secure the asset.

Although the dog could easily retrieve the ball, barking for backup was his way of bringing me into his game. "I'm coming, Duke."

As I jogged along the path past a beagle and a pair of playful poodles, an overwhelming sense of dread fell over me. I broke into a cold sweat and couldn't get enough air. I placed my hand over my chest and tried to breathe, but my body was tense with fear, and I couldn't calm my racing heart.

I knew then that something happened—or will happen— to Leo.

I grabbed my phone and called him.

No answer.

I called his partner.

Straight to voice mail.

I reached into my bag and grabbed my sketchpad. I hadn't had a premonition for months. If this was what I was experiencing, I needed to warn Leo about the impending danger.

"Duke, come!" The dog obeyed and ran to me.

I clipped on the dog's leash, forced myself to breathe, and headed home to draw.

OFFICER DOWN—LEO

"**O**fficer Down!"

Footsteps thundered toward me.

As I lay on the ground, stunned, a hand lifted my wrist and checked for a pulse.

"Hang on, Leo. Help is on the way."

I blinked to chase away the stars flashing before my eyes. My vision was blurry, but I made out the face of the man beside me. Parker—my partner on the Violent Crimes Task Force.

I lifted my head and tried to get up, but Parker placed his hand over my chest and told me not to move. The throbbing pain in my head made me too weak and disoriented to argue. It felt like someone had cracked my skull with a baseball bat.

"Do you know what happened? Did you see who hit you?"

Parker leaned over me with his gun drawn, ready to engage. While he surveyed the scene, he rattled off a series of codes to Dispatch and relayed the address of our location.

I tasted blood in my mouth, and my ears were ringing louder than the sirens nearing the building. I racked my brain and tried to answer Parker's question, but a round of vertigo forced me to shut my eyes to stop the world around me from spinning.

"Stay awake," Parker demanded. "Paramedics are on the way. What is the last thing you remember? Leo?…Leo?…"

My attention drifted to a woman lying beside me. She was wearing my old Loyola t-shirt. Her legs were bare, and she wasn't wearing any shoes. I couldn't make out her face through my blurry vision, but I noticed abrasions and bruises around her wrists.

Her identity was a mystery, but I felt a sense of duty to protect her.

"Are you in pain?" I asked, motioning to the ligature marks on her wrists. I was certain I never intentionally harmed a woman, but the guilt swirling in my gut told me I was responsible for her injuries.

"Always." She leaned over my injured body and kissed my lips. Her long hair spilled over my face like a sandy brown curtain.

"Fight for me, Leo." She ran her fingers through my hair to soothe my aching head. I still couldn't make out her features, but the scent of her skin and the familiarity of her touch led me to believe she was someone close to me.

The woman grasped my hands and pressed them to her heart. "Open your eyes, Leo. Stay with me."

"Detective Ricci, can you hear me?" A male voice shouted.

I snapped out of my dream or memory or whatever it was and blinked in confusion as a team of medics surrounded me. While I lay on the cold, hard ground, the crew asked me a bunch of questions.

"Do you know what happened to you?" one guy asked.

"I think I hit my head."

"Are you hurt anywhere else?"

"No, but there's another victim here." I searched the faces

hovering over me, but the woman was no longer beside me. "Parker, there was a woman here. Is she okay?"

"I didn't see a woman. What did she look like?"

"Nice legs. Long fingernails. Ligature marks on her wrists. She was wearing my old Loyola shirt from college."

"I know who you are referring to, but she was never here."

"Who is she?"

Parker's expression turned serious. "Sounds like you're describing Evelyn."

"Who is Evelyn?"

BANG—EVELYN

I raced home when I couldn't reach Leo or Parker.

I grabbed my sketchbook and art supplies, spread out a blanket on the floor, and took a series of calming breaths to clear my mind from distractions. I focused on Leo and willed the universe to give me something I could use to help him.

I had no control over my gift and had no idea what my automatic drawings would produce, but I was desperate for information to save Leo from whatever was happening.

My body trembled as I considered why I sensed Leo was in danger and what I would discover when I used my paranormal gift.

Had Leo been killed in the line of duty?

What if the sickening feeling in my gut stemmed from death? There were only two reasons why I had this overwhelming urge to draw. The universe was trying to warn me that something bad would happen to Leo, or that the tragedy had already come to pass.

The thought that I might sketch Leo as a ghost filled me with terror. I conjured up images of Leo as a restless spirit and envisioned his ghost haunting me in my dreams. If Leo died suddenly from a violent act, I feared he would remain earthbound to connect with me in my dreams and through my art.

No. This can't be happening. Calm down, Evelyn. Leo needs your help.

I inhaled a series of deep breaths and focused all my energy on Leo. Once I calmed my mind and body and found myself in a meditative state, I held my pencil in the ready position and waited for the spirits to guide me.

As I concentrated on the man I love, my hand moved across the page.

Bang, bang, bang!

A heavy fist pounded on the door, startling me out of my trancelike state. I inhaled a sharp breath and opened my eyes as I snapped back to center. Duke barked at the door to alert me we had a visitor. I dropped my pencil and hopped to my feet to find out who was there.

When I stood up, I studied the drawing in my sketchbook. I'd drawn a wolf in the woods, peeking around a tree under the light of a full moon. There was a shadowy figure lurking in the shadows, but nothing else significant stood out.

What did this have to do with Leo?

Bang, bang, bang!

"Evelyn! Open the door. It's me," Officer Santoni bellowed. He was Leo's best friend since childhood, and he'd become like a brother to me over the last year.

Fear coursed through my veins as all the what-if scenarios raced through my mind. Something horrible had happened to Leo—I felt it in my bones. Leo's team had sent Santoni to track me down to deliver bad news.

I clutched my drawing and raced through the living room to meet the messenger. When I flung open the door, Santoni held out his hands as if he meant to calm me before I succumbed to a panic attack.

"What happened to him? Is he dead?" Tears streamed down my cheeks as Santoni clutched my upper arms to keep me from falling over. My legs turned to rubber as I waited for Leo's fellow officer to deliver the tragic news that Leo had been taken from me.

"Evelyn, listen to me. Leo is alive. He was injured in the line of duty, but he's at the hospital now. I'm going to take you there. Do you understand?"

I nodded as I grabbed my purse and jumped into my shoes. "What happened? Who hurt him? Is he going to be all right?"

"We don't have all the answers yet, but Parker is with him now. All we know is that someone knocked him pretty good on the back of the head."

I gasped at the mental image of my brave boyfriend being attacked. Leo was a strong man and dangerous in his own right. He was a trained law enforcement officer and obviously carried a gun. The thought that someone had snuck up on him and bashed him in the head—I held my stomach as acid came up my throat. "Tell me he's going to be okay. We can't lose him."

"Leo is a fighter, Evelyn. He'll get through this. All we can do now is pray and be there for him when he wakes up."

Hang on, Leo. I'm on my way.

KNOCKOUT—LEO

My ears were ringing louder than the ambulance sirens.

Parker stayed by my side as we raced to the hospital. According to my partner, an unknown assailant had snuck up behind me, cracked me in the head with a blunt object, and fled the scene.

The blow had left me knocked out for several minutes, but now that I was awake, all I wanted was to escape from the ambulance and hunt down the son-of-a-bitch who had gotten the jump on me.

But the stars flashing before my eyes and my throbbing headache were textbook signs I had suffered a concussion. As much as I wanted to get back on the case, I barely had the strength to lift my head off the gurney.

Once the medics transported me to the hospital, the emergency crew wheeled me into the ER to run some tests. Parker refused to leave while the medical staff poked me and questioned me about my injuries.

I told everyone who would listen that I was fine. I just

needed to rest for a couple hours, then I would be as good as new.

No one bought that story.

A physician wearing scrubs and thick glasses entered the room and introduced herself as the ER doc. She pulled a penlight out of her jacket and shined it in my eyes. During the examination, she asked a series of obvious questions:

Who is the President of the United States?

What did you have for breakfast?

What month is it?

What year?

When I responded to her last question, the doctor gave me a funny look. "Could you repeat that, please?"

When I gave her the answer, she smiled politely and turned off her penlight. "What is the last thing you remember? Do you know why you are in the hospital?"

Her line of questioning annoyed the hell out of me. I knew with a hundred percent certainty what year it was and didn't like the way the doctor was treating me like a school kid who didn't know the capital of Illinois.

"The last thing I remember was..." I wanted to prove the doctor wrong, but the details were fuzzy.

My head was throbbing, and I had an ice pack under my head to ease the pain. For the life of me, I couldn't remember a single detail about the attack—or my attacker. "You said someone hit me, right?" I looked at Parker for confirmation.

"That is the assumption. You went to the park to meet a witness, Cora Bradford—Professor Nolan Bradford's wife. You asked me to hang back while you spoke to her, because she wanted to talk privately first," Parker said.

"We were separated when the crime occurred, so I don't know for certain how you sustained your injury," Parker said. "We were hoping you could tell us what happened."

"Focus, Detective Ricci," the doctor said. "Take your time and tell me the last thing you remember."

My frustration level was reaching the tipping point. I was done with all the questions and wanted to get the hell out of this hospital so I could think things through without all the pressure. There was too much commotion going on around me, and I couldn't concentrate.

"What do I have to do to get out of here? Do I need to sign some papers or what?"

The doctor patted my arm. "I will get you discharged as soon as I can, Detective. However, after my exam, I can confirm you are suffering from a concussion. You'll be here overnight, at the very least."

"No way, I can't stay here. I have to—"

"Leo!" A gorgeous young woman with long golden-brown hair rushed into the room. She cupped my cheeks with her clammy hands and stared into my eyes. "Are you okay?" Streaks of mascara ran down her cheeks, and her eyes were red from crying.

"What happened? I've been so worried about you?" She gave me a visual frisking, then kissed my forehead. When she leaned in, her perky breasts brushed against my arm, and her long hair tickled my cheek.

This woman, whoever she was, certainly knew me, but I'd never seen her before in my life. There was no way I would forget a knockout like her.

"Leo, say something. You're scaring me." Her beautiful blue eyes were laced with concern.

"Do I know you?" I asked.

Her expression tanked. "Please don't make jokes right now, babe. Just tell me you're okay."

"I'm not joking. I don't believe we've ever met."

Her eyes widened in panic, then she shifted her gaze between Parker and the doctor, searching for answers. When neither of them spoke, she turned her attention back to me. "Leo, it's me. Evelyn. I'm your girlfriend. You don't remember me?"

Girlfriend? The room started spinning as my brain tried to process what this woman—Evelyn—was saying. I didn't know what was going on or why some lady was in my hospital room pretending we were a couple.

The only thing that made sense was that maybe we had a one-night stand, and she thought that meant we were dating. That seemed delusional—especially since I didn't even recognize her.

I shot my gaze to Parker for clarification. I rarely spoke to him about my personal life, but maybe he could bring me up to speed on my relationship with her. We may have known her from a case, or maybe she worked at the precinct.

"Do you know her, Parker?"

He gave me a nod. "I do. Evelyn and I are good friends."

What the fuck? I turned my attention back to Evelyn.

She was as pale as a ghost.

LOST—LEO

After I failed my examination, the doctor cleared Parker and my girlfriend out of the room and set up more tests.

The good news was, physically I was okay. I had a concussion that required me to rest, but other than that and a couple of scrapes and bruises, I had no other injuries.

The real problem was my memory.

After hours of questions and a shitty night's sleep, the doctor returned in the morning to update me on my condition—in addition to the concussion, I also had amnesia.

In my current state of mind, I was living in the past. The last thing I remembered was working a murder investigation with Parker and my team—the Sloane Matthews case.

When I'd given the doctor key details I could share about my ongoing investigation, she consulted with Parker, who confirmed the information. According to the timeline, my memories were from last fall.

I lost an entire year of my life.

That explained why I had no memory of my alleged girlfriend—Evelyn Sinclair. According to Parker, we had met shortly after that time, but I didn't have a single memory of the woman I was supposedly madly in love with.

With all the bizarre stuff that was happening, I needed to work this out with my best friend. Santoni and I had been buddies since birth, and if anyone could help me sort through this shitstorm, it was my old pal who knew me better than I knew myself.

Once the doctors and medical staff stopped interrogating me and left me alone for five minutes, Officer Santoni burst into my room. "You look normal enough to me—grouchy and impatient as ever," Santoni joked, giving me a mental break from the emotional trauma.

Past him, I could see there was an officer stationed outside my room. Damn. That likely meant the officer was guarding my room because whoever had attacked me had not yet been captured.

Santoni turned serious when he informed me that my family had all been notified and were at the hospital, waiting to visit me as soon as I felt up to it. For now, I requested no visitors. Before I could see my loved ones—or Evelyn—I needed to get up to speed on what was going on in my life.

"How are you feeling, Leo?" Santoni asked.

"Confused," I said.

"You lost an entire year?" Santoni asked.

"That's what they tell me."

"But it's only temporary, right? Your memory is going to come back after you get some rest?"

This was the one question the doctors couldn't be certain of. "They said my amnesia may only be temporary, but that there's a chance I will never recover my lost memories."

Santoni leaned back in his chair and exhaled dramatically. He stared up at the ceiling as he considered how to respond.

This guy was a brother to me, and I knew he was struggling to come up with the right thing to say.

My situation was bad, not only on a personal level, but on a professional one, as well. I would never get cleared to get back to duty until I got the green light from my doctor. What if this memory loss was significant enough to sideline me from being a detective?

My badge was my life. The idea of losing the one thing that defined my character and gave me a purpose in this crazy world had me reeling. How would I live without my career in law enforcement?

That was probably what my old friend was thinking. He was a uniformed officer who took his job as seriously as I did. He would be equally worried about his career if he were in my position.

"Talk to me, buddy," I said. "How bad is this?"

Santoni straightened his shoulders and looked me dead in the eyes. "This is fixable—even if you don't get your memory back. You guys are indestructible. Nothing will keep you apart. Not even this."

You guys? I slow-blinked like a dimwitted animal. "What are you talking about? Who's indestructible?"

Santoni's eyes softened as he regarded me with pity. "You and Evelyn. I swear to God she will help you get through this."

I hated this fucking hospital. I hated being injured. And I hated being trapped by a woman I didn't remember. "Fine. I have a girlfriend. I'm sure she's very nice, but right now, I need to concentrate on getting the fuck out of this torture chamber so that I can get back to work."

I hopped out of bed, pressed the call button to summon the nurse, and grabbed the clear plastic bag that held my clothes. I had a pair of pants, shoes and socks, but my shirt was missing. I vaguely remembered the medics cutting it off me in the ambulance. As I put on my pants, Santoni watched me incredulously as I prepared to make my escape.

"Hang on a second, Leo."

"I'm leaving," I snapped.

"You know I'd take a bullet for you, right?"

"What's your point?"

"I'll bust you out of here if that's what you want. I'll do anything you ask me to do. You're my best friend, and I love you, man, but—I need you to do one thing for me in return."

Getting the hell out of the hospital was my priority. Santoni was my ride-or-die buddy, and I knew that whatever he was about to ask came from his heart. "What?"

"Hear me out. That's all I ask."

I gave him a nod of agreement.

"Evelyn is not just your girlfriend. She is not some woman you hang out with casually when you have time off. She is your entire life, buddy. If you had to choose between her and your job, you would turn in your badge without blinking."

"I think you're the one who got hit in the head. My badge is everything. You know that."

"Leo—"

I put up my hand to silence him as I processed how I was going to get through this. I trusted Santoni, but I couldn't imagine having these feelings for Evelyn or anyone else. The last woman I remembered seeing was Rochelle, a smoking hot Italian beauty who hung out in our local dive bar.

I never "dated" the women I spent time with. My job always took priority. My social calendar would never sync up with my cases. Chasing killers took precedence over date nights, neighborhood barbeques, and all the things that went along with being in a committed relationship.

Falling in love was never an option for me.

If Evelyn and I were as serious as everyone seemed to think, how was it possible I had no memories of her? I believed Santoni was trying to steer me in the right direction, but how could he know how I felt about another person?

"Look," I said. "I know you're trying to help, and I will take everything you said into consideration. But all I want right now is to get the fuck out of here and get back to—"

A nurse in blue scrubs bustled into the room. When she saw me out of bed with my belongings in hand, she planted her hand on her hip and cocked her head. "Where do you think you're going, Detective Ricci?"

"You need to unhook me from all this crap so I can get out of here." I motioned to the IV drip, and the tubes and wires attached to incessantly beeping machines.

Instead of following my instructions, the tough old gal shook her head in defiance. "I don't take orders from you. When the doctor says you're good to go, then I'll unhook the crap, got it?"

Her attitude was justified, so I changed my tone. "Listen, I respect you have a job to do, but I'm leaving this place with or without your help. Can you please unhook me or do I need to do it myself?"

"No." The fed-up nurse aimed a finger at my chest. "But since you asked so nicely, I will get the doctor and let you plead your case to someone who can help you."

On her way out the door, she looked up at Santoni. "Don't let your friend do anything stupid, Officer. If he yanks out that IV and bleeds all over this room, you're cleaning up the mess."

"Yes, ma'am." Santoni touched the brim of his hat and gave her a nod.

A few moments later, a doctor wearing a freshly pressed white lab coat entered the room with a clipboard in hand.

"I'm Dr. Abrams, the top head trauma specialist in the city. I'll be taking over your case. How are you feeling, Detective Ricci?"

This new doctor sure was full of herself, but I was glad I had the top head doc in Chicago.

"I need to get out of here, Dr. Abrams. Can you sign the discharge papers or whatever you need to do to speed this along?"

The doctor pushed her designer glasses up her nose and studied my chart. "I would like to keep you here for observation for at least another night. Your memory loss concerns me in addition to your concussion. Brain trauma is serious, Detective. You'll need around-the-clock care during your recovery."

"You said I needed rest. I can't do that here. Let me go home and sleep this off. Once I get a decent night's rest, I'm sure my memory will come back."

"Do you live alone, Detective?"

"Yes."

Santoni shook his head, contradicting my statement. "You don't live alone anymore, buddy."

"Who do I live with?" I said through gritted teeth. I was sure I already knew the answer, but the last thing I wanted to hear was her name again.

"You and Evelyn moved in together last year." Santoni shifted his gaze to the doctor.

"You live with Ms. Sinclair?" The doctor seemed to be up to speed.

"I guess I do."

"Don't worry. Evelyn will take good care of him, doc. She's the only one this stubborn guy will listen to."

Since I would not be home alone, the doctor agreed to sign my discharge papers. I got what I wanted, but it floored me that not only was I in a committed relationship, I had let my girlfriend move in with me, too.

While I mentally kicked myself in the ass, someone knocked on the door.

"Leo? Can I come in?" Evelyn said.

Speak of the devil.

UNMATCHED—EVELYN

I was relieved to see Leo standing by his bed and talking to the doctor, but when I entered the room, he seemed irked that I was there. Santoni excused himself so Leo and I could talk to the doctor.

"Hey, Leo. How are you feeling, babe?" I opened my arms to give him a hug, but he didn't reciprocate my show of affection. I lowered my arms and fidgeted with my long, gauzy scarf.

"Great," he said. "The doctor is getting the paperwork ready so that I can get out of here."

I placed my hand over my heart and sighed with relief. "That's fantastic news. Thank you, Dr. Abrams." I pulled a fresh stack of Leo's clothes out of my tote bag and handed him a shirt.

He gave me a nod, grateful I had thought ahead, so he didn't have to leave the hospital half-dressed.

I ran home this morning to get my car and clean up before facing him again. There was so much going on, I needed to be his rock. I wanted Leo to see me as the strong and resourceful person I had become over the last year.

No more crying. No more pity party. Leo needed me to be brave while he healed from his injuries. As the doctor explained the discharge instructions, Leo watched me out of the corner of his eye.

He studied my dainty beaded earrings and long layers of crystal necklaces. His gaze wandered down my body as he checked me out. I had changed into jeans, tall suede boots, a soft white t-shirt, and a one-of-a-kind scarf designed by yours truly—my usual artsy style.

He squinted at my ghoulish scarf from my Ghosts in the Graveyard collection. I suppressed a smile as Leo scrutinized the undead design of restless spirits mingling among the tombstones.

He had to be thinking—why the hell am I dating this spooky chick? I wasn't like the other women from Leo's past. Before me, he spent time with the heavy makeup, tight clothes, push-up bra brand of beautiful women.

My natural look and casual style were the opposite of the ladies he normally found attractive, but the sexual chemistry and attraction between us were unmatched. I wasn't worried Leo would reject me because of my spooky vibe—he loves me.

Give him time, Evelyn. Leo will get his memory back soon.

"Do you want a prescription for pain meds?" Dr. Abrams asked.

"I don't take drugs." Leo snapped, eager to finish up.

"Evelyn, I understand you will be the caregiver. Questions?"

"Dark room, lots of liquids, peace and quiet, no driving, and take him to all his follow-up doctor appointments. Got it." I pulled my key fob out of my purse, mirroring Leo's not-so-subtle signal we were ready to bolt.

If I had accomplished one thing today, I hoped I proved to Leo that I always had his back. No matter what.

STRANGLED—EVELYN

As I drove home from the hospital, my heart felt like it was about to explode.

I was stunned by Leo's diagnosis of amnesia and leveled by the reality that I was a complete stranger to the man I loved. Quite a turn of events from where we started yesterday morning.

When the doctor broke the news to me about Leo's condition, she said his memory might come back in a day, a week, a month—or never. Mentally, I had to strike that last option off the list and concentrate on helping him recover as quickly as possible.

Freaking out, coddling him, or showing signs of weakness would drive Leo further away from me. Parker had been with me when the doctor explained Leo's condition and offered advice on how to handle our latest crisis.

Stay calm. Don't try to force him to remember. Be yourself.

On the drive home, I kept the conversation to a minimum. He had to have been in a lot of pain, but my tough-as-nails boyfriend would never admit it. I turned the air to arctic blast mode the way he liked it, and strangled the steering wheel to relieve my mounting stress as we headed home to our apartment.

Leo studied my white-knuckle grip on the wheel. "How are you doing with all this?"

I relaxed my hands and forced a smile. "Life is never dull with you, Detective. Just another obstacle we have to overcome."

"Another obstacle? What else happened that we had to get over?" Leo's head injury may have blurred his memory, but his detective's brain was as sharp as the tip of a knife.

Be cool, Evelyn. The last thing Leo needs to hear right now is the truth about our tumultuous past.

"Oh, you know. Nothing in particular. Just life stuff." I forced a laugh to keep it breezy.

Leo studied my stiff body language, surely searching for tell-tale signs I was being deceptive. Maybe when we got home to our apartment, Leo's memories would resurface, and life would go back to normal.

"What kind of life stuff?" Leo prodded.

It was impossible to evade Leo's interrogation. I wanted to tell him everything about the last year. How I narrowly escaped the clutches of The Windy City Stalker, and how we both survived a tangle with the notorious Chicago Mob.

But I couldn't tell him all the details about my involvement in his case now. That would lead him to ask more questions about why I had become involved in his murder investigations and why I never seemed to keep myself out of trouble.

Whatever happens, Leo can't find out about my paranormal gift.

The truth almost destroyed us the first time he learned I could communicate with the dead. I had to hang on to hope that his memory would return before he asked the wrong questions.

Questions that could derail our relationship.

When Leo and I first met, he didn't believe in ghosts. How would he react if I had to explain my gift to him now that I was a complete stranger? Knowing his aversion to paranormal phenomena, he would think I was a fraud—like he had in the past.

"What do you do for a living?" Leo changed up his line of questioning.

"I'm an artist. I have a gallery on Halsted in the Arts District."

"Interesting. You look artsy." Leo's gaze drifted to my ghostly scarf. "Did you design that?"

"Nice work, Detective." I tossed him a smile.

His gaze lingered on my chest, and I doubted he was admiring my scarf. "How did we meet, Evelyn?"

I stopped at a red light. I gave Leo all my attention as I prepared to tell him the story of us. "We met at a coffee shop near my gallery—Taboo."

"Yeah, I know the place. What happened after we met? Did I drop a pickup line on you? How did I convince you to go out with me?" Leo's frown lines softened as he waited for me to elaborate on our chance encounter.

This is good, Evelyn. Lighten the mood a little.

"Not exactly." My cheeks warmed with embarrassment. It was surreal that Leo had no memory of our fateful encounter, but a rush of excitement washed over me as I prepared to share the details of our romantic history.

"I always draw in the morning while I enjoy my coffee. I pick something random that catches my attention and sketch. On the morning we met, you caught my attention."

For the first time since his injury, Leo gave me a little

smile. I took that as a good sign. He may not remember me, but our mutual attraction was undeniable.

The light turned green. As I followed the line of traffic, I explained how he'd busted me drawing his portrait, the fiery exchange that followed, and how he walked me back to my gallery under the guise that I should never walk alone in the city.

"So when it was time to say goodbye, what happened? Did I ask you out then or ask for your number?"

I shook my head and laughed. "No. I asked you out. I invited you to my art show the following Friday."

At that point, my cheeks were on fire, and I thought I might die from embarrassment.

"Did I go?"

"You did."

"Really? I'm not an art show kind of guy. I must've really liked you to go to something like that."

"You could say that." Leo laughed along with me when I told him how we made out in my studio during my debut art show, and how he had playfully threatened to cuff me and lock me in his interrogation room if I failed to answer his questions."

"Nice. Very charming. Did I follow through on that threat?"

"Not on the first night, Leo."

Leo's eyes smoldered with desire. "But we did eventually go there?"

The story was skidding dangerously close to entering Windy City Stalker territory. We were almost home, and I needed to buy some time before Leo continued asking questions.

"Not yet. I'm still a virgin."

Leo lifted his eyebrows. "You're a what?"

I cracked up at my stupid joke. "Sorry, I'm just messing with you."

Leo chuckled as he pointed to the road ahead. "You need to get in the right lane. It's easier to get to my place if you turn here."

My heart sank when I realized he didn't remember where we lived. This detail was one of many he had lost. "You don't live in the old neighborhood anymore. We moved into an apartment together near the gallery."

"I sold my house and moved into an apartment? Why the hell did I do that?"

A tsunami of guilt washed over me, knowing I was the reason.

THE TRUTH—LEO

$\mathcal{E}$velyn was keeping something from me.

Her body language was rigid, and she was trying her best to fool me into believing everything was cool. If we had been together for a year, then she had to have known that trust was the foundation of all my relationships.

When Evelyn parked her car in front of what I assumed was our apartment building, she turned off the ignition and gave me a hopeful smile. "Welcome home, Leo."

Failing to be honest with me was a deal breaker. If there was something Evelyn needed to tell me, she better cop to it before I found out on my own. In fairness, I had zero memories of our relationship. The entire last year of my life was a mystery.

I didn't expect her to tell me everything that happened from the moment we met at the coffee shop through today, but if there was something major I needed to know about her or us, I wanted to hear it sooner rather than later.

"Oh, I forgot to answer your question about why we moved into this apartment." Evelyn's tall leather boots clicked on the sidewalk as we headed to the entrance of the building. "It was your idea. You surprised me. We moved here so I could be closer to my gallery."

The decision to sell my house and throw away my hard-earned salary on rent seemed way off the mark for me. I would run all this information past Santoni to make sure Evelyn was telling the truth, but it would be stupid of her to lie about this, knowing I would check out her story.

"Anything else I need to know?" I wanted to give Evelyn an easy path to filling me in on whatever it was she was keeping from me.

She touched my arm and fixed her baby blues on mine. "I have a million things to tell you, Leo." She paused and took a deep breath. "You are the most important person in my life, and I love you so much. My heart is torn in half right now, and I'm trying my best to keep it together for your sake." Tears welled in her eyes.

"I know it's impossible for you to trust me right now, but I swear all I want in this world is to help you recover so you can get back to work and we can be us again. I will do anything and everything in my power to make that happen."

In my line of work, I was trained to detect lies. As I stared into this gorgeous woman's eyes, there wasn't a trace of deception. Her sincerity leveled me, and even though I had no memory of her, Evelyn Sinclair knew me. It was clear she was trying to put a brave face on while respecting my need for the truth.

The pain in her eyes wrecked me. I reeled her in and gave her a reassuring hug. The petite young woman curled herself into my arms, buried her head in my chest, and molded into the contours of my body.

"We'll get through this, Evelyn. Thank you for sticking by me." I kissed the top of her head and inhaled the comforting scent of her citrus shampoo.

Evelyn rubbed her hand on my back as she took a couple

of deep breaths to calm herself down. Then she fished a set of keys out of her purse and led me to the entrance "Oh, there is something you need to know before we go inside."

Here we go. Whatever was on the other side of that door was the thing she was keeping from me. Whatever it was, it had to be big, and I believed I knew what she was trying to hide. "Evelyn, give it to me straight. Do we have a kid?"

"No!" Evelyn burst out laughing. "I wouldn't leave our baby alone in the apartment."

Instead of explaining, she opened the door. I was surprised to find a smiling furry face there to greet me. "We have a dog?"

"Only for a few more days. This is retired K9 Duke. We're dog sitting for your friend, Officer Campbell. She's on her honeymoon, and we volunteered to keep him."

"Hey, buddy. I remember you." I patted the dog on the back. "Campbell and Duke helped us locate a missing woman a few years back. If it wasn't for the search and rescue team, we may not have found the victim alive."

Evelyn kissed the dog on top of his head, then kicked off her boots and left them beside the door.

I scanned the room, hoping to find something familiar that would help me regain my memory. There was a big white sofa in the living room loaded with about nine-hundred throw pillows.

On the coffee table, there was a long metal tray that held a collection of candles and crystals and random little trinkets. The scent of essential oils filled the air, and there were decorative baskets filled with yoga props and fuzzy blankets littered all over the room.

"Does anything look familiar?" Evelyn asked hopefully.

"Not yet." I moved to a bookshelf along the wall that held a library of thick art books and stacks of sketchpads like the one I saw in her purse when she was digging around for her keys.

I picked one up and was about to flip through the pages, but Evelyn touched my hand to stop me.

"Sorry, those are private."

"Then why do you keep them on display in our living room?" It was a fair question, considering they were out in the open where anyone could access them.

"You respect my privacy. I don't have to hide them. We trust each other, Leo." Evelyn gave me a gentle smile, hoping to avoid a conflict.

Evelyn was an artist. Why didn't she want me to see her art?

She had her own gallery in the famed Arts District on Halsted Street. What was the big secret hiding in her sketchbook?

Instead of grilling her, I let it go.

All I wanted was a hot shower to wash the hospital smell off my skin and a moment to myself to process all that had happened over the last day and a half. "This is our bedroom?" I pointed to the door just past the dining room.

I headed for the door, but Evelyn jumped in front of me and blocked me from entering.

I was sick of surprises and losing patience with her evasive maneuvers. "Is there something in there you don't want me to see, Evelyn?"

"No." Evelyn cracked a smile. "I just want you to be ready to see it."

What could possibly be in our bedroom that I had to be ready to see? Judging by the clutter around our apartment, Evelyn wasn't exactly a neat freak. I predicted our bedroom was a mess, and she hadn't had time to clean up before I got home. "I'm a homicide detective, Evelyn. I'm sure I can handle whatever is in there."

Evelyn stepped aside and allowed me to enter our room. When I opened the door, Evelyn was right—I wasn't ready for this.

SPOOKED—LEO

There was a painted version of us making love.

Our nude bodies glistened with sweat. Evelyn had painted her perky breasts a luscious shade of peachy pink. The painted version of me grasped her hips from behind as I thrust inside her, and she immortalized our expressions of ecstasy on the canvas.

While it shocked me to see the erotic painting on our bedroom wall, I had to confess her art turned me on. Evelyn was still a mystery to me, but one thing had become crystal clear—she was the sexiest woman I've ever met.

"Fucking hell." I side-eyed Evelyn. "You're an erotic artist? Was this on display for the entire city to see at your gallery?"

Evelyn waved her hand as if she could erase my response. "No, Leo. This painting is just for us. You and I are the only ones who have ever seen it. My artistic style is supernatural. Angels, heavenly beings…ghosts."

"Ghosts?"

"I'm known as the spooky artist on Halsted. You're my biggest fan, Leo. You come to all my art shows. When you're feeling up to it, I'll give you a tour of the gallery."

Since when did I give a flying crap about art? I did a visual sweep of the rest of the room and zeroed in on a collection of framed photos lined up on the dresser.

Me and Evelyn at Nona's birthday party. The two of us snuggled up at a hockey game. Evelyn holding up a picture of me she had drawn in her sketchbook. As I stared at the snapshots of our lives, nothing seemed familiar.

I was a tough guy trained to remain calm in high-pressure situations, but this memory-loss crisis was reaching critical capacity. I was still me, but I felt trapped in someone else's reality. From the moment I got admitted to the hospital, my friends and family had been trying to convince me how much I loved Evelyn.

But how could I stand here in our erotic playground and feel nothing for the woman I was allegedly in love with?

All this new information was making my head spin. I needed to focus on something familiar—the Sloane Matthews investigation. Her missing person case felt as though it had happened only yesterday. Our investigation may have stalled over the last year, but the details were fresh in my mind.

Since I was now sidelined on medical leave, I could focus on the college girl's case to keep my mind active. "I need to go over my case files. Do you know where I keep them?"

Evelyn's complexion paled. "Yes. We use the spare bedroom as your home office. Your work files are in the safe."

"Great. Thanks for your help."

"Sure, no problem, but—" Evelyn wrestled with her thoughts. "Don't you think you should rest?"

"No. I think I should get back to work." When I reached my office, I was pleased to find this space was all mine. No scented candles or decorative throw pillows. No pictures or art or stacks of forbidden sketchbooks.

I had a gun safe, a desk, my comfortable couch from the old place, and a large industrial safe with a digital lock that held my private work files. I ran my hand over the keypad.

What the fuck is my passcode?

I tried a couple of numbers I'd used in the past, but none of them cracked the safe. I slammed my fist down on the top in frustration.

Dammit! Why can't I remember anything?

Stressing myself out wouldn't help my cause. I recalled the doctor's advice that rest and relaxation was the best medicine. Maybe if I could calm myself down and get a decent night's sleep, my problems might resolve themselves by the morning.

Evelyn gave me some space after I left my office, and I was grateful to have a moment to myself finally. The mounting stress was taking a toll on my mental health, and I needed to decompress after all the drama and confusion I'd been experiencing since the attack.

I cranked up the heat in the shower and inhaled the steam as I processed the events over the last twenty-four hours. I had no memory of the attack. No suspects. No way of knowing who had it out for me.

Whoever attacked me is still on the loose.

As I lathered up my body, I focused on how I would handle my domestic situation with the gorgeous stranger I was about to crawl into bed with. Evelyn had a rocking body —if she had painted herself accurately—and the new me seemed to really enjoy her company.

My best friend believed Evelyn and I were a solid couple. The photographic evidence and the erotic painting in our bedroom supported that theory. I'd also sold the house I loved to move into an apartment with Evelyn so she could be closer to her gallery.

These were the undisputed facts.

So why was I having a hard time trusting her?

I may not have my memories, but my gut was telling me she was hiding something. She got spooked when I asked questions about her art. It seemed strange that a professional artist didn't want her boyfriend to see her drawings.

Why was she being evasive? She clearly wasn't shy about hanging a pornographic painting in our bedroom. What could she have drawn that would've been more personal than that?

Evelyn's indignant response echoed in my head. "We trust each other, Leo."

PLAYTHING—EVELYN

I'm going to lose him.

I was deceptive when Leo asked me questions.

Strike one.

I changed the subject when he asked me why we had moved into our apartment.

Strike two.

I lied when I told him my drawings were personal, and I trusted him not to look at my sketches.

Strike three.

I was doing everything wrong, and Leo was catching on to my lies. I needed to turn this around before my boyfriend decided he didn't want to be around me. Once Leo opened his safe, he would find pictures of me as a victim, along with my gory and disturbing drawings of the dead in the Windy City Stalker files.

God, how can this be happening?

I heard the shower water running and figured Leo would open his safe after he cleaned up. Unsure of what to do, I took care of the dog and then changed into my nightgown.

It was too early for bed, but I was emotionally wrecked. I

needed a moment to calm my body and mind before Leo discovered my secret. I curled up on the bed with a throw blanket and picked up a novel. I wanted to look casual, so Leo would believe everything was cool.

Another lie.

When Leo emerged from the bathroom, a cloud of eucalyptus-scented steam escaped the room. He was shirtless, wearing just athletic shorts, and his skin was hot pink from the shower.

His muscular body rocked, and if he hadn't just been released from the hospital, I would've pounced on my sexy man and dragged him into our bed.

"How was your shower?" I asked.

Leo's gaze dropped to my chest, drifted down my body, and then landed on my legs. He loved my firm and toned body, compliments of yoga, and seemed distracted as he admired my bare skin. "You look…comfortable."

I recognized the hungry look in my boyfriend's eyes and knew his thoughts had taken a detour down a sexy path. I rolled on my side to give him a glimpse of my body from another angle and smoothed my hand over the bedspread.

"Come to bed, babe. I'll give you a massage while your muscles are all warmed up."

A sexy grin curled on his lips as he slid into bed beside me. "A massage sounds nice." He propped a couple of pillows behind his head, no doubt because he was in pain.

I didn't want to baby my strong-willed man, but I hoped he had taken an over-the-counter pain reliever as the doctor had suggested. Rest was what he needed more than anything, and I wanted to help him relax.

I ran my long fingernails over his muscular arms, lightly scratching his skin. Leo's early-morning workouts and healthy lifestyle earned him a firm and well-defined body that drove me wild. His strong will and commanding presence matched his chiseled abs and thick arms.

I reached into our special drawer, where we kept our bedroom toys, and pulled out a bottle of warming lotion. As I rubbed a generous pour of strawberry-scented oil into my hands, Leo's eyes were wild with desire. I sat on my knees beside him and slid my hands over his chest, focusing my massage on his shoulders.

Leo kept his gaze on mine as I pushed my long hair aside to keep it out of the way. While my hands glided over his warm skin as I kneaded his muscles, the tension lifted from his body. Leo exhaled a deep sigh of relief as his body relaxed.

My touch was new to him, but I had the luxury of knowing exactly what my man liked. Over the last year, Leo and I had become more than lovers and best friends. Our relationship had reached the pinnacle status of soulmates.

While I massaged him, the strap of my silky white nightgown fell over my shoulder. I started to slide it back up, but Leo touched my hand and stopped me.

He offered a sexy smile and caressed my skin as his gaze lingered over bare breasts visible through the sheer fabric. "Where did you get this?"

"You bought it for me. It was a gift to celebrate our first night in our new apartment."

He eyed me skeptically. "That was a very romantic gesture. It doesn't sound like me, though. What else did I do?"

I blushed at the memory. "You were full of surprises that night. Dinner at home, a bottle of wine, and—some other little things." I tapped him playfully on the chest.

"Trust me, Leo. You are the kind of guy who loves to surprise me. After a good night's sleep, you're going to wake up and remember all of our wonderful memories."

"What other little things did I get you?" My inquisitive boyfriend asked.

I bit my lip and shifted my gaze to the drawer where we kept our intimate toys. "Oh, just some—" I laughed and pointed to the dresser. "We like to play around, you know, with battery-operated things?"

His eyes were wild with desire. "I hope I tell you how incredibly sexy you are every fucking day, Evelyn."

I squeezed his biceps and turned away, embarrassed by his flattery. "Yes, babe. You are the best boyfriend in the world. You don't just tell me, you prove it every moment we are together. Leo, everything you do is for us."

Leo wasn't thinking about his memory when he slid the thin strap of my nightgown down and exposed my breast. "Let me prove it to you now, Evelyn."

Feeling oddly shy, I touched his hand and slid it away. "Leo, the doctor said you need to rest."

I pulled the strap of the nightgown back up and covered myself. "Besides, we just met—I mean, you just met me. I'm practically a stranger to you."

"That's what makes it exciting. I want to make love to you for the first time—again. Say yes, Evelyn." Leo rolled on his side and kissed me deeply. He smoothed his hands along the curve of my silhouette and slid my nightgown up my thigh, enticing me to give in to his sexy request.

Feeling the warmth of his body and his rough, unshaven cheeks scratching my skin seduced me into giving in to Leo's desires. "Yes," I whispered, as I ran my fingers along the waistband of his shorts and slid them off.

Leo groaned excitedly and pressed his body against mine. Warm ripples of pleasure pulsed in my core as he trailed kisses down my neck and pulled my nightgown down.

He brought each breast into his mouth, sucking and swirling his tongue around my nipples as his muscular body weighed down on me. Leo's strength and alpha control excited me, and I was ready for whatever he had in mind.

Our lovemaking was never routine, and I was curious about how Leo would take me our "first" time. His head must've been aching, but his desire to make love to me outweighed his pain.

"God, Evelyn. Your body is amazing." Leo reached into the drawer and found our secret toy stash. A moment later, he snuggled up behind me, and the familiar hum of one of our sex toys vibrated between my legs.

My body reacted to his touch as he rubbed the toy over my intimate zone and sucked on my neck as I purred with erotic passion.

"Oh, Leo. You feel so good." My back arched against his chest as I moaned softly. My sexy lover never failed to please me, and I was on the verge of letting go.

"Give it to me, Evelyn," Leo growled.

I panted Leo's name as I came undone and dug my fingernails into his thigh as I climaxed. When my body relaxed, Leo tossed the toy aside and gave me an intimate massage.

"God, Evelyn. You're so wet. What am I going to do with you?" He nibbled on my ear as he slid his finger inside me, exploring a deeper region of my erogenous zone. His erection poked me in the backside as he pleased me, kicking my excitement up to the next level.

"I'm ready to go again." I swiveled my hips and placed my hand on his, encouraging him to go faster. Leo was a fantastic lover and always brought me to orgasm multiple times. Once he got me fired up, I could go all night.

Leo understood my desire and took me there once again. I let out a breathy exhale as my body tensed, and warm ripples of pleasure spread across my core. Leo instinctively knew how to please me, and I was eager to return the favor.

I rolled on top of him, pinned back his muscular arms,

and straddled his abs. I lifted his hand to my mouth and sucked the sweetness of my body off his fingers. Leo's smoldering gaze burned with desire as I scooted down and rubbed my body against his rock-hard erection.

I slid his fingers out of my mouth. "How do you want me to take you, babe? I'm all yours." Leo eyes were wild with lust as he considered my request. I was a stranger to him, and the loving expression he normally had for me was no longer present.

We were not making love—this was just sex for him. Knowing this was only a temporary situation, I didn't mind letting Leo treat me like his own personal plaything—as long as I knew we would get back to normal soon.

"I've got you right where I want you, gorgeous. I want you to ride me." While I was on top of him, Leo moved my body into position and eased inside me.

The sensation of his enormous erection took my breath away. "You're so big, Leo. I can feel every inch of you." I groaned as my body stretched to accommodate him.

"You're so fucking sexy, Evelyn." Leo grasped my hips and encouraged me to bounce as he thrust deeper inside me. His grip was firm as our bodies synced up into an erotic rhythm.

My breasts bounced wildly from our fast and furious, erotically charged ride. The bedsprings squeaked. The headboard banged against the wall. Our moans and sexy sounds echoed through our bedroom.

During our energetic lovemaking, I came undone for a third time that night. Leo groaned with pleasure as he climaxed along with me. As we came down from our sexual high, I collapsed on the bed.

"Do we always have this much fun?" Leo panted.

"Every night, babe."

"Damn."

HAUNTING—LEO

Evelyn was sound asleep, but I was too wired to close my eyes.

Her long golden hair fanned out over my chest and our naked bodies were intertwined in the world's most perfect sleeping position.

Her warm skin and gorgeous body had me excited and ready to go again. While I was deeply attracted to my wildly sexy girlfriend, I felt no attachment to her. The sex was great, but as far as I was concerned, we had just met yesterday.

If I stayed true to my nature as a carefree bachelor, I would've slipped out of bed and been out the door before Evelyn opened her eyes. I loved keeping company with beautiful women, but I never let my personal relationships interfere with my badge.

But since Evelyn and I lived together, I couldn't exactly run off and leave without saying goodbye or leaving a note. I stared at the ceiling fan as it whirled overhead and replayed our intimate moment, then shifted my gaze to the dresser and studied our photos.

When I had first seen the pictures, I focused on Evelyn.

This time around, however, I considered my reaction to her. The tender way I looked at her made the non-committal bachelor in me cringe. In one photo, I was so locked and loaded on the woman in my arms that there was no other way to describe my reaction to her other than love.

How did you let this happen, Ricci?

Carefully, I slipped out of bed without waking her. I went to my office and grabbed my phone to see if anyone from my team had tried to reach me.

Aside from a string of well wishes from my fellow blue bloods, friends, and family, I got a text from my partner.

PARKER: Hope you get some rest. Let's meet tomorrow and discuss your case. Let me know if you or Evelyn need anything.

I glanced at the clock. It was too late to call him back. I had a lot of questions about my attack, but they would have to wait until the morning.

My most pressing concerns all revolved around Evelyn. I couldn't shake the nagging feeling that she was keeping something from me. My files and laptop were locked in the safe, but I didn't have to be a cop to do an internet search and learn more about her.

I typed Evelyn's full name into the search. I expected the first hits that would come up would be about her gallery or her career as an artist, but—holy shit.

LOCAL ARTIST SURVIVES SERIAL KILLER

Below the news headline, there was a haunting black-and-white photo of Evelyn taken in front of her art gallery, along with photos of the killer's other victims who had not survived.

I skimmed the article to understand what had happened and how Evelyn had escaped from the clutches of a madman. While I got up to speed on the number of victims and the facts provided in the article, I learned that the killer had stalked all the women before they were abducted.

Including Evelyn.

There were many details missing from the story that I needed to look into, but one important fact jumped out: Parker and I were the lead investigators on the case.

I got out a paper and pen to create a timeline of events. Evelyn and I met a year ago—before the crime occurred. My team had taken down the killer a few weeks after that, which meant…Evelyn and I were dating during the time of her abduction.

The killer targeted Evelyn because of me?

As I skimmed the articles and jotted down key details, rage came over me when one of the news outlets posted a photo of Evelyn's attacker, the Windy City Stalker. When I read about how he had committed his heinous crimes, I wanted to punch something to relieve my anger.

This is Evelyn's secret.

The kind and loving woman sleeping in my bed doesn't want to tell me I failed to protect her from a deranged killer.

How the hell did I let this happen?

I would ask Parker to fill me in on the details of the crime. But with Evelyn—I would wait to bring it up until I understood the facts. She was the victim, and I respected her decision not to talk about it.

I'm sorry I didn't protect you, Evelyn.

CREEPY—EVELYN

Tap...tap...tap...

Someone knocked on our bedroom window, waking me from a deep sleep.

I sat up in bed and searched for Leo, but he wasn't there.

"Leo?" I called.

No answer.

I tossed off the blanket and got out of bed, but when my feet touched the floor, I stepped into something wet. I looked down and found myself standing in a pool of blood.

A thick, red river oozed from the window and flooded our room. As I stood there horrified, a woman appeared behind the glass. Moonlight broke through the trees and illuminated the woman's face.

Her ghastly pale skin was blotched with blood splatter, and her matted dark hair clung to her face with a combination of mud and dark streaks of dried blood. That's when I realized the woman was no longer alive—this is a dream.

She was hiding something behind her back, but I couldn't see what it was. "Who are you? What do you want?"

When the woman realized I could see her, she showed me

what was behind her back—a bloody axe. As she hovered outside our bedroom, she raised the axe and slammed the blade into the glass, shattering the window.

I cried out in vain for Leo as the woman crawled through the jagged glass and rushed toward me. The sudden movement caused her severed head to tilt off her shoulders and dangle from her body, attached only by a few stringy veins and skin.

Frozen with fear, I was helpless to protect myself against the ghost as she pinned the blade of the axe against my throat. The scent of burned wood, musty earth, and death oozed from her decaying skin.

With her head dangling, she fixed her gaze on mine and hissed violently—the only sound she could make with severed vocal cords. She was trying to tell me something, but it was impossible for her to communicate.

This is a dream, Evelyn. Wake up. Wake up!

I bolted upright in a cold sweat, panting with fear. I placed my hand over my heart, and as I came down from my nightmare, a word popped into my head.

Aurora.

I had the overwhelming feeling that this dream was somehow connected to Leo's attack. I couldn't explain how or why I had this feeling, but all I knew for certain was I needed to draw.

I got out of bed and searched for Leo. He wasn't home. Since the dog was not in the apartment either, I reasoned Leo had gotten up early and taken the dog for a walk. While I was alone, I grabbed my sketchbook and pencil, went back to our bedroom, and locked the door.

The last thing I needed was for Leo to come home and find me in the living room, drawing for the dead. I propped a couple of pillows behind me and tried to relax. I inhaled a series of deep, cleansing breaths, cleared my mind of distractions, and held the tip of my pencil to the page, ready for my gift to take over.

Once I found myself in a meditative state, my hand moved across the page.

WHEN I OPENED MY EYES, I checked the clock. An hour had gone by, and if Leo had come home during that time, he must've thought I was still sleeping and didn't want to wake me. I was relieved I didn't get caught, but then as I glanced down at my drawing, an unsettled feeling crept over me as I studied the details in my sketches—three drawings total.

The first one featured a beautiful young woman dressed up in a sexy Little Red Riding Hood costume. She had long dark hair, big brown eyes, and a slice across her throat as if someone had tried to decapitate her.

This is the woman from my dream.

The next drawing featured a raging bonfire. At first glance, nothing unusual stood out. But upon closer inspection, there were body parts and bits of bones and teeth hidden in the design.

The gory sketch revealed a melted human face with deep black holes in place of the eyes and dismembered limbs with long, painted fingernails with Halloween motifs. While the first two sketches seemed related—a homicide victim and burned remains—the last drawing threw me off.

The last sketch was of a creepy Victorian doll collection. There must've been over fifty dolls, each with unique features and different fabric designs on their dresses. They seemed well-preserved for their age, but they were all piled in a heap, and it seemed the dolls had been discarded.

What did these drawings have to do with Leo's attack?

GUILTY—LEO

I texted Parker an hour ago, but I still hadn't heard from him.

I was an early riser, and even a concussion couldn't force me to sleep in or skip a morning workout. I had crashed on the couch in my office after finding out about the serial killer, and Evelyn was still in bed when I left to walk the dog, so I slipped out without waking her.

I was glad to have some time to process what I had learned about her last night. Everyone in my inner circle loved Evelyn. She was a wildly successful artist, adored by her fans, and respected by her peers. The photos of us in our home told a happy story.

So why did I have the unshakeable feeling something strange was going on with her? I could accept that Evelyn was keeping information about the Windy City Stalker case from me because she didn't want to stress me out, but there was something else. I could feel it. I checked the time. It was 8:00 a.m. Still no reply from Parker.

What's going on, Parker?

I hoped that there had been a lead in my case, and he was busy making an arrest. I needed something solid to happen. It was unnerving knowing my attacker was still on the loose. I made a mental list of the possible suspects.

A felon from the past coming back to seek revenge? A suspect connected to one of my current investigations? All I knew for certain was that someone had it out for me. It was a bold move to attack an armed man who carried a badge.

Now that the tables had turned, and I was the victim of a violent crime, I wasn't permitted to play an active role in the investigation. All I could do was give my statement, make a list of people who might have a vendetta against me, then do nothing and wait for a break in the case.

Sitting on the sidelines during an investigation went against my grain. I was a leader. Hanging back while my team investigated my case would eat me alive.

I rechecked my phone.

Dammit, Parker. You better be reading someone their rights.

I switched gears and turned my attention to the dog. "You ready for breakfast, Duke?"

He looked up at me with his big brown eyes and wagged his tail. He had no idea what I said, but even though he was retired, he was still a working animal at heart and always ready for action.

We passed the coffee shop where Evelyn and I had met, so I went in to get something to go. I had no idea what she liked, so I ordered a safe-bet plain bagel with cream cheese and a black coffee for her. I ordered a protein smoothie for myself, then headed home.

When I entered our apartment, it surprised me to see Parker there with Evelyn. Her sketchbook was between them on the table along with her pencil case—she shows her draw-ings to him, but not me?

The two of them looked guilty as sin.

"Good morning, Leo. I got your message and thought I would find you here," Parker said. "How are you feeling?"

"Fine."

"Hey, babe. How was your walk?" She gave me a peck on the cheek, then greeted the dog.

I handed her the bakery bag and coffee. She seemed elated that I had gotten her breakfast, but when she checked inside the bag and realized what I had picked up, her elation tanked. "Thank you. That was really thoughtful."

"Did I interrupt something?" I shifted my gaze between them.

"I was just interviewing Evelyn about what she remem-bered from the coffee shop yesterday morning. She was with you when you took the call from Cora Bradford."

"Didn't you already interview her?"

"Yes, but we were all a bit rattled at the hospital, so I wanted to go over the facts one more time." He tapped a pen over the notebook he used when he interviewed witnesses.

"What do you remember?" I asked Evelyn.

"You were off duty. We had plans for the day, but when the call came in, you felt it was urgent enough that you needed to meet her."

"What plans?"

"I don't know. You were going to surprise me."

Another fact that seemed out of character for me.

"What happened next?"

"You said you would be back in an hour, called Parker, then rushed out the door," she said. "That's it. I don't know what happened after you left the coffee shop."

I turned my attention to Parker. "Have you located Mrs. Bradford?"

"No. According to her friends and family, she left town after her husband's affair went public. She's been out of touch, and her family doesn't know where to reach her. If she was indeed back in Chicago, you seem to have been the first person she contacted, Leo."

"What about Professor Bradford? Have you interviewed him?"

"Also gone. He left town a few months ago. He lost his career, his wife, and the respect of his colleagues. He and Cora had no children and nothing tying them to the city. Looks like the couple went their separate ways."

I thought about the update on the Bradfords. "The last thing I remember was bringing him in for questioning about Sloane's disappearance. Did the professor ever get charged with a crime?"

"No. He admitted to having an affair with his student but claimed to have no information about her disappearance. We couldn't prove otherwise, so we never charged him with a crime."

"Has that changed?" Evelyn asked. "Has there been a development in the case?"

Parker shifted his gaze to Evelyn. "I can share details that have circulated in the news," Parker said. "Nolan Bradford claimed to have been home the evening of Sloane's disappearance."

Evelyn listened carefully as Parker went on.

"Leo was adamant Nolan was involved in her disappearance, but the DA said we didn't have enough evidence to charge him."

"What evidence did you have?" Evelyn asked.

"We found blood, a patent leather shoe, and an article of torn clothing from the costume Sloane was last seen wearing. Nolan's car was also identified at the scene. We found love notes from Sloane when we searched the vehicle that confirmed the affair. We found DNA in the vehicle, but he admitted to having sex with her in the car."

"No news about Sloane?" I asked.

"No," Parker said. "Her whereabouts remain a mystery."

Evelyn crossed her arms nervously as Parker and I discussed the case. Maybe hearing about Sloane's disappearance struck a nerve, considering she was a victim of a violent crime herself.

"Evelyn, we can talk about this in private if it makes you uncomfortable."

She looked up, surprised. "No. I want to know as many details as you can give me. Someone hurt you, Leo. If Nolan Bradford is after you—"

"What makes you think the professor is after me?" I shifted my attention to Parker.

"We don't have much to go on, but we had an eyewitness come forward about your attack. She was at the park when the crime took place and saw a man matching Nolan's description fleeing the scene after your assault."

"Did she make a positive ID on the professor?"

"Unfortunately, no," Parker said. "But I need to remind you that he was furious at you, in particular, for ruining his life. All along, he's claimed his innocence, but you never gave up on him as your prime suspect in Sloane's disappearance."

"Do you think he's the one who attacked Leo?" Evelyn asked.

"I don't know," Parker said. "But the professor publicly blamed Leo for ruining his life. News crews caught up with the professor as the investigation lingered." Parker pulled up a news archive on his phone and shared the clip.

"Detective Ricci is the guilty one. He cost me my career and tarnished my reputation in this city. He needs to be held accountable for his crimes against me."

Nolan Bradford aimed his finger at the news camera.

"You can't go around accusing innocent people of crimes they didn't commit, Detective Ricci. You ruined my life. I won't let you get away with it."

Holy shit, the professor really had it out for me.

"Keep your eyes open," Parker said. "Nolan Bradford is a person of interest."

I hated keeping secrets from Leo.

Especially now that I understood someone had a vendetta against him. When I realized the woman in my dream was Sloane Matthews, I called Parker immediately to update him.

I sent him my horrid automatic drawings, along with the sketch of the wolf peeking around the tree I'd drawn at the time Leo had been assaulted. The idea that the main suspect in Sloane's disappearance was also a person of interest in Leo's attack frightened me to the core.

Why had Cora Bradford contacted Leo? Did the professor's wife have information about Sloane's disappearance? Did she have evidence against her husband?

The bigger mystery was, why was Nolan coming after Leo now? If he had left town, why did he come back? And why had he decided now was the right time to come after Leo?

It seemed the case had stalled. Sloane had been missing for a year. Her body had not been found, and there were no charges against Nolan. For a supposedly smart man, it seemed incredibly stupid to attack a big guy with a gun in a public place because of an old grudge.

Something must've happened that lured Nolan back to town, but what? While I didn't have all the answers, I knew for certain Leo was in danger.

I wanted to tell him everything, but I remembered how the detective had handled my gift the first time I tried to explain it—he didn't believe me. Dropping the paranormal bombshell on Leo while he was recovering was not in his best interest.

I wasn't sure how to handle it, so I had a group meeting with Parker and Santoni about it while Leo was in the hospital. This was too important of a decision to make on my own, and I trusted my friends to steer me in the right direction.

The three of us decided it was best not to reveal my secret —not yet, anyway. The doctor said Leo could get his memory back at any moment, and we all hoped that would happen sooner rather than later.

While Parker was at our apartment, updating us on Leo's case, my phone buzzed with a string of incoming texts. I ignored the messages, but after my phone kept buzzing, I checked to see who was trying to reach me—my gallery manager, Gibson.

"Do you need to answer that?" Leo asked.

I shook my head and stuffed my phone into my pocket. "No, it's just work calls. I have an art show coming up. My gallery manager has some questions, but I can deal with this later."

"Right. You've missed the last couple days of work to take care of me," Leo said. He seemed put off that his traumatic injury had kept me from my job.

"Because you needed me. I want to be with you, Leo. Work can wait."

Parker glanced at his watch. "I need to run. I'm tracking

down a few more leads." He headed to the door. "Stay safe. I'll update you when I can."

When Parker left, Leo grabbed his jacket. "Are you ready to give me a tour of your gallery? I can visit while you check in with your staff. Sound good?"

I was surprised Leo wanted to tag along while I went to work, but I knew him better than he realized. The detective had questions about me, or us, and believed he would find the answers at my gallery.

MISSION—LEO

My doctor said that rest and relaxation were the best medicine for my recovery, but I had taken a different approach. I would do whatever it took to regain my memory as soon as possible.

I asked Evelyn to take me to her gallery for a reason—other than I was curious about her art. Apparently, we spent a lot of time together there. I hoped by visiting familiar places, my brain would reboot and my life would go back to normal.

When we got to Halsted, the first thing that stood out about Evelyn's gallery was the name—The Death of Me, An Evelyn Sinclair Gallery.

Inside, ghostly figures, an army of dark angels, and a self-portrait of my hot girlfriend painted as a corpse greeted me as she gave me a tour of her gallery.

Evelyn's macabre style and morbidly accurate depictions of death were a stark contrast to her calm and cool demeanor. The post-mortem details in her painting portrayed the hauntingly beautiful artist as a restless spirit, unwilling to accept her fate.

As I cruised the gallery and studied her work, Evelyn trailed along beside me as I scrutinized her latest collection, The Devil in Disguise. Her talent was beyond anything I had ever seen. Evelyn snuck glances at me as I toured her gallery, waiting for me to say something.

I didn't know much about art—or the artist—but Evelyn seemed to have a fascination with ghosts and death. Blown away by her talent, all I could think to say was, "Damn. I've never seen anything like this. Your art is next level, Evelyn."

She tossed me a grateful smile. "Thanks, Leo. You've always been supportive of my unique style."

"Good. I'm glad to hear that." I walked back to her self-portrait and aimed my finger at the painted, corpse-version of Evelyn. "Have you always had a fascination with ghosts?"

Evelyn shook her head. "I started painting a few years ago. I was involved in an accident that changed my life."

"What happened?"

"I died."

"You what?"

Evelyn went on and told me a story about how she drowned in a lake and was clinically dead for several minutes before first responders resuscitated her. She was in a coma for days, and when she pulled through, she started seeing ghosts in her dreams.

"The near-death experience changed me. When I came back to the land of the living, I had a new appreciation for the afterlife. Ghosts who visit me in my dreams inspire my art," Evelyn said.

Her story about surviving a near-fatal accident floored me. Now I understood her obsession with death, but I needed clarification on the ghost thing. I wanted to be certain I understood how she perceived her otherworldly encounters.

"I need some clarification on these ghost dreams of

yours." For reference, I pointed to a morbid painting of a corpse wearing a wedding gown. "Walk me through the process. Do they just show up, or do they want something from you? Do they reveal their cause of death? Guide you to their crime scenes? Lead you to unmarked graves?"

"That's a lot of questions, Detective," Evelyn laughed. "I'm glad you're interested in my art. Let me show you my studio upstairs." She started to leave, and I got the feeling she didn't want to answer my question.

"Personally, I don't believe in ghosts and want to make sure I understand your perspective on the subject. So, the only time you see ghosts or have any contact with them is in your dreams? You sleep, and you see ghosts. You wake up, and they're gone, right?"

"Pretty much. There's really not much else to say."

Pretty much was not the right answer. "Wait. I need to understand something. Do you believe these ghosts in your paintings are real?" I asked. "Listen, if you put on this ghost story stuff to promote your work, I don't have a problem with that. But when you're talking to me, I don't want slippery answers or half-truths or make-believe stories you come up with for your art fans, alright?"

Evelyn gave me a knowing smile. "This feels like a déjà vu moment, Leo. We've had this conversation before. I have an artist's soul. I believe something becomes real the moment I produce it in my mind," Evelyn said.

"When I create my art, the subjects are forever immortalized on the canvas. I can't separate my art from my life for you or anyone else. I hope that makes sense."

In my line of work, I would never let anyone get away with a bullshit answer like that. Evelyn wasn't guilty of a crime, but she sure was being evasive about her art. More than ever now, I was convinced she was keeping something from me, and I made it my mission to find out what it was.

SCANDAL—LEO

hile Evelyn hung back at the gallery to work with her team, I dove back into the Sloane Matthews case.

Even though a year had passed since Sloane disappeared, the details were fresh in my mind, as if the crime had happened yesterday. I opened the case file and spread the folders and photos across the table.

I studied the police report filed by Sloane's roommate Lindsey that stated she had not returned to the dorm for three days, which ultimately led to Sloane's classification as a missing person.

Lindsey also revealed that Sloane had confided in her about her relationship with the professor and had given her intimate details about their kinky sex life. The professor was into role-playing and liked to get a little rough.

My team and I considered the professor may have killed his student during sex by accidental strangulation or asphyxiation. These types of accidents happened, and it was something we had to consider. The professor may have disposed of her body to cover up the crime.

I looked over the witness statements from the bonfire—her last known location. Several friends confirmed she was there, wearing a Little Red Riding Hood costume. No one saw her leave the party. It appeared she vanished sometime during the evening.

I looked for consistency in the reports, and only her roommate had knowledge of her affair with Professor Bradford. However, two witnesses stated they saw the professor's car at the park that night.

I studied the photos of Nolan's older model, 1992 Volvo 240 Sedan. Not a rare car, but it was a classic. White with black trim, block headlights. Even though we had solid statements that his vehicle was on the scene the night Sloane disappeared, no one could confirm that they had seen the professor at the party.

The other piece of evidence we had was an envelope with a stack of pictures of Sloane at various places on campus. Someone had sent it to her, but there was no note or return address. The package also contained a hair tie, a receipt from a restaurant, and a ticket stub from a ball game.

Years of experience led me to believe Sloane may have had a stalker or a misguided suitor who believed it was romantic to track her movements and keep tabs on her every move.

I opened Nolan Bradford's person of interest file. I studied a collection of photos of the smiling professor, adored by his students, friends, and faculty. He wore book-themed t-shirts featuring portraits of famous authors and notable book quotes scrolled across the center, along with a blazer, jeans, novelty socks, and leather loafers.

His dark-rimmed glasses, braided leather bracelets, vintage watch, and wavy shoulder-length hair matched his reputation as a "cool college professor." The students described him as charming, passionate, and an all-around nice guy.

Even "nice" guys take advantage of young, impressionable women.

When Parker and I interviewed Nolan, he claimed he was innocent of any crimes but admitted to having an affair with Sloane. When we questioned him about his alibi, he stated he was home that evening and did not know why witnesses claimed to have seen his car there.

Nolan got tight-lipped, however, when my partner asked him why he thought Sloane had dressed as Little Red Riding Hood that night.

AGENT PARKER WILLIAMS: "Did you and Sloane ever discuss Little Red Riding Hood or fairytales? Was she a fan of the Brothers Grimm? Did you engage in cosplay or rough sex?"

NOLAN BRADFORD: "No."

When Parker mentioned Sloane, Little Red, and rough sex in the same sentence, Nolan clamped his mouth shut. From that point on, he answered all our questions in a yes or no sequence and refused to elaborate on more details when pressed.

I believed the Professor was being deceptive, but our biggest concern was finding Sloane. A year had passed, and no one had seen her since the night of the bonfire. With no remains, no evidence of a crime, and no confession, Sloane was still a missing person.

As I flipped through my witness reports, I stopped when I came across Cora Bradford's statement. According to the professor's wife, Nolan was home that evening as he claimed.

CORA BRADFORD: "He was in his study reading, as usual. His light was on, and his dull classical music records were playing in the background. My husband prefers to be alone after dinner, and that evening was no different than any other night."

DETECTIVE LEO RICCI: "Are you aware your husband is having an affair with Sloane Matthews?"

CORA BRADFORD: "That's a lie. My husband would never cheat on me. Nolan has many faults, but he is a faithful man."

DETECTIVE LEO RICCI: "I have a witness testimony that states otherwise, Mrs. Bradford. The affair started at the beginning of the fall semester. Has your husband been leaving in the evenings, staying out late, making up excuses to leave the house?"

Cora dismissed the accusation, but as she denied her husband's infidelity, Parker and I had both picked up on her body language. She fidgeted nervously in her chair and fussed with the hem of her blouse, smoothing out the wrinkles and picking at a stray thread that had come undone at the seam.

There was something off about her demeanor. When we turned up the heat about her husband's affair, she sobbed and became extremely emotional as she professed her husband's innocence. Sure, she was under a lot of stress, but her emotional outburst didn't fit our line of questioning, and I didn't believe her melodramatic antics for a second.

The bright and dutiful wife defended her husband's honor as she lied through her teeth. In a situation like this one, there were three reasons an upstanding citizen would cover for a cheating spouse.

The first was pride. Cora was a well-loved English professor's wife. Her home was filled with framed photos of the happy couple from a decade's worth of happy memories. A cheating scandal would wreck her perfect life, and lying to protect her marriage seemed like a reasonable motive.

The second reason was that Cora knew her husband had

not been home that night, and she was creating an alibi for him. That would be a huge mistake, but if she believed he was innocent, she might lie to protect him.

The third reason Cora would lie was the most damning. She knew her husband was guilty, but was covering up for him. My gut was telling me she was lying, and I made it my mission to find out why.

That explained why I had agreed to meet Cora at the park —alone. I was hoping she was ready to come clean and tell the truth. Then we would finally find out what happened to Sloane Matthews—the college freshman from a small town who disappeared from a party without a trace.

HONESTY—EVELYN

*L*eo still had not regained his memory. I wanted to remain calm, but I feared Leo might never recover from the year's worth of memories he had lost.

I made a reservation for dinner out of town where no one knew us. A quiet, romantic place where Leo and I could spend time alone without pressuring him to remember his life—or worrying about who had a vendetta against him.

On the off-chance Leo's memory never returned, I wanted to make new memories and restart our relationship on a positive note. I was an eternal optimist and never wanted to consider the worst-case scenario, but I sensed Leo's initial red-hot attraction to me was cooling off.

He knew I was hiding something.

The last thing I wanted to do was for him to see me as an anchor, dragging him away from his career or a burden on his domestic freedom. The people he loved and trusted the most kept telling Leo I was his dream girl. But he needed a reason to believe it for himself.

As I drove us out of the city, Leo drummed his fingers on his leg, something he did while he was trying to figure things out. After he left the art gallery, he met with Parker again. I was certain they discussed the case that brought us together.

"I did some research last night. I learned a lot about you," Leo said.

"Everything has been happening so fast, and we haven't had time to discuss our lives, past and present. That's why I want us to spend time together tonight so we can talk things out."

Leo gave me a nod of acknowledgment. "Parker answered a lot of questions about the Windy City Stalker case today, but I wanted to hear the truth straight from you."

"The truth about what?" I tried to remain calm and trust that Parker would've given me a heads-up if he had dropped the paranormal bombshell on Leo today, but the idea that Leo had found out about my gift made me nervous.

There were two versions of my near-death experience—the one I discussed publically about ghosts visiting me in my dreams, and the secret I held back about how ghosts came to me to help them find peace.

The version Leo got today was the one I discussed freely at my gallery. I was open about the fact that I dreamed of restless spirits, but there were only three people in the world who knew the true nature of my gift—Leo, Parker, and Santoni.

Now that Leo had lost his memory, his best friend and partner were my only allies. My gift was too dangerous to reveal to the public, and Leo wasn't ready for the truth.

Leo's expression turned serious. "Why were you involved in my murder investigation?"

"My friend Sydney Reynolds was one of the victims. I got involved to help you track down her killer."

"Why did I let that happen? You are a civilian. There's no reason I can come up with that I would let you put your life on the line to solve the case."

Confession time. Leo deserved the truth, but telling him something this big in the car, while I was driving, was all wrong. We needed to be face to face for this. Eye to eye. No distractions.

"That's correct, Leo. I shouldn't have gotten involved. You did everything in your power to stop me from playing junior detective, but I didn't listen. My stubbornness to stop the killer nearly cost me my life." Not a lie. Just not the whole truth.

I veered off the highway exit that led to the restaurant, then pulled into the lot and parked the Audi by the entrance. "I want to answer all your questions and help you understand why things happened the way they did. We can stay up all night and talk if that will help ease your mind."

Leo gave me a nod and seemed relieved I was willing to be open with him about his concerns. "Thank you, Evelyn. I appreciate your honesty."

I leaned over and gave him a kiss. "I love you, Leo. I'll do everything I can to help you through this."

BURNED—LEO

The host seated us at a cozy table by the window. Evelyn looked beautiful in the ambient candlelit restaurant.

The flickering flames and fall décor put off a warm and welcoming vibe, and the change of scenery lifted our spirits. Life had been so hectic since the attack, and I was relieved to have some time with Evelyn to come down from all the trauma.

We ordered a round of drinks and apps, then I gave Evelyn all my attention. She looked amazing in a curve-hugging sweater dress and mile-high stilettos. She styled her long hair in loose, cascading curls and put on a touch more makeup than she'd worn since I'd met her.

No. That was a stupid thought. I met her more than a year ago.

Amnesia is so fucking nuts.

Evelyn was a certified knockout, and my gorgeous girl-friend attracted a lot of attention, but her gaze never wandered far from mine. She was proving to be a loyal and loving companion, and now that she was ready to open up and answer all my questions, our relationship seemed to be going in the right direction.

All I wanted from her now was the truth. The nagging feeling in my gut that Evelyn wasn't being honest with me was still there. I hoped in our talk this evening, we could clear the air.

Evelyn admired the warm and inviting setting as she sipped her wine. She must've been feeling as lost and helpless as I did, and I appreciated that she was trying her best to make the best of a life-altering situation.

"This feels like a first date," I said. "Do we go out often?"

She smiled and brought her attention back to me. "We love to go out. I often work in the evenings, and your schedule is never predictable, but we always find time for our date nights."

"Damn. I sound like an amazing boyfriend."

Evelyn leaned forward and touched my hand. "In every way imaginable, babe."

Now that we had a break from all the stress, Evelyn and I could relax and enjoy our date night. The conversation never paused as we bounced from one topic to the next.

She talked about my family as if she had known them for years. She filled me in on all the birthday celebrations and family gatherings with my siblings I'd forgotten and described the people I loved in such detail that I felt as though I never missed a beat.

As we noshed on appetizers, Evelyn scooted her chair next to mine, pulled out her phone, and showed me pictures of us on a romantic beach vacation, tons of photos of us at her gallery, and a year's worth of solid, feel-good memories with the people I loved.

"I can't wait for you to remember your birthday party this year," Evelyn touched my arm and smiled. "I was feeling ambitious and had this big idea that I would bake a cake for your party. I invited everyone to our place to celebrate, so I wanted to make it extra special and surprise you with a homemade birthday cake."

"Sounds nice. What flavor did you make?"

Evelyn shook her head and blushed as she described how she wanted the cake to be big enough to serve all the guests, so she used two cake mixes and poured them into one pan.

I loved seeing her complexion glow as she recalled her horror baking story. Her blue eyes lit up as she poked fun at herself while giving me a glimpse into our domestic lives.

"I didn't realize that the cake would rise so much, and when it did, it spilled out of the pan and dripped into the oven. I started a freaking fire in our kitchen, Leo!" Evelyn squeezed my arm as she cracked up at her honest mistake.

"CFD had to come to our apartment to put out the flames. I was so embarrassed, and when I explained what I was doing and who I was baking the cake for, the guys razzed you mercilessly when you came home. It was brutal, babe," Evelyn said. "I was so grateful I hadn't burned down the building that I invited the whole fire crew to the party."

She pulled up more photos on her phone and shared pictures of all my friends, old and new, raising their beers in salute. "All things considered, the party was a blast."

Every picture Evelyn shared led me to the same conclusion. My best friend was right.

Evelyn is my world.

By the time the dessert course arrived, the walls I'd put up around Evelyn had crumbled down.

I admired Evelyn's adoration for my family and friends, and her sense of humor and the adorable way she told her stories gave me a reprieve from the stress I'd been going through since my attack.

Evelyn slid her plate of cherry cheesecake between us so we could share. One thing I'd noticed about her—she loved sweets. Evelyn slid her fork into the decadent dessert and let out an mmm as the sweetness spread across her tastebuds.

As the creamy dessert melted in her mouth, Evelyn flinched and her eyes widened in surprise as if someone had come up behind her and startled her.

"Are you all right, Evelyn?"

She shifted her gaze around the room, scanning the faces of our fellow patrons. She seemed alarmed by something or someone, but nothing had happened as far as I could tell. Everything appeared to be business as usual in the dining area.

"Is something wrong?"

Evelyn remained calm, but her body language was rigid. "Snake eyes."

"What?"

"Does that mean anything to you?"

"No. Why would it? What's wrong with you?"

"I need you to trust me, Leo. I promise I have a good reason for asking." She forced a smile and sipped some water in an attempt to act normal. "Has anyone ever said those words to you? Does it have anything to do with any of your cases?"

"Not that I can remember." Evelyn was acting really weird. A second ago, we were talking about her upcoming art show, then suddenly—whap! She flipped into a paranoid disaster.

"We need to leave. I'm going to put some cash on the table to cover our bill. We need to go straight to the car. I know this is a strange request, but once I explain what is happening, you'll understand."

Evelyn slid a pile of cash on the table and then headed for the door. Maybe she had a possessive ex-boyfriend or a crazed fan obsessed with her otherworldly art. Based on what I read about her in my research, Evelyn was a local celebrity in the art world, and she obviously attracted a lot of attention because of her edgy style and alluring beauty.

I didn't know what she had seen or heard or experienced that spooked her, but I was on her heels in a hot second, ready to protect her. As I tailed Evelyn to the car, that inkling of doubt I had been feeling about dating Evelyn came roaring back and was now a giant yellow caution flag.

There was seriously something wrong with Evelyn Sinclair.

When we got into the car, and Evelyn rolled out of the parking lot, I saw the shadow of a man behind the wheel of a car parked in the back of the lot. The vehicle pulled into traffic behind us and tailed us for a couple of miles before pulling off the exit.

Evelyn and I were silent as she drove back to the city. She promised to tell me everything when we got home, which gave me time to process everything that had happened. Snake eyes. What an unusual thing to say.

Evelyn promised it would make sense once she explained it, but I couldn't fathom how or why she cut our perfect evening short because of it. As I racked my brain and tried to come up with an explanation or a source for the phrase, I eventually made a connection.

Professor Nolan Bradford had a pair of fuzzy dice hanging from the rearview mirror of his Volvo—the same car that witnesses identified on the scene at the bonfire where Sloane Matthews was last seen.

The interesting thing was, we had a warrant to search his car after Sloane disappeared. I had gone over the photos of the vehicle in my case file and recalled the position of the dice—double zeros—snake eyes.

TRUST—EVELYN

Once Leo and I were behind closed doors, the interrogation began.

"No more games. No more secrets. Whatever you've been keeping from me, it all comes out now." Leo looked exhausted and fed up, and I hated to go down the paranormal path when he clearly needed to rest.

"There's something about me I haven't told you yet. It's shocking, and I was hoping your memory would return before I had to explain it to you all over again."

There was no way to soften the blow or sugarcoat what I had to say. Leo was right to be upset and confused by my strange behavior, but I feared that once I tried to explain my gift, things would only get worse.

I thought I'd be able to tell him tonight, but I was wrong. This wasn't the time. This would blow everything up, and I'd lose him for sure. He hadn't recovered enough to deal with this. It was hard enough to get him to believe me the first time. No, this was not the moment. Not yet.

"Talk to me, Evelyn." Leo picked up my hand and led me

to the couch, an attempt to soften his tense demeanor. "Whatever your secret is, I can handle it."

I lit a trio of candles on the coffee table and stared at the flickering flames as I summoned my courage. "The foundation of our relationship is trust. We made a promise to never keep secrets from each other, no matter the consequences."

"Good. I wouldn't have it any other way," Leo said.

I fidgeted with the fringe on my throw pillow. "With that said, I'm going to ask you to trust me. I only want what is best for you, and telling you my secret now will do more harm than good."

Leo stared at me, stunned by my response.

"All I ask is for one more night. If you get a good night's sleep, maybe your memory will come back in the morning, and we won't need to have this conversation. The doctor said rest is the best medicine—"

"What are you afraid of, Evelyn?"

That was the most straightforward question of the night. "Losing you."

I remained silent as Leo's gaze sharpened on mine. "How can you deliver this speech about trust, then twist it to suit your needs? Why don't you trust me? Tell me the truth about whatever it is you've been keeping from me since I laid eyes on you at the hospital."

Leo got off the couch and paced the room. "What is it about me that stops you from being honest? How bad is this secret? If you're afraid to tell me because you might lose me, what the hell did you do?"

"I didn't do anything, Leo. It's late. I don't want to argue. We had such a good time tonight, I don't want to ruin it—"

"Fine. I'll wait to have this conversation in the morning— if you answer one question for me."

"Okay. What is it?"

"Why did you ask about snake eyes tonight?"

Here we go—the unanswerable question. "I'm sorry. I can't answer that right now. Trust me—"

"No, Evelyn. You need to trust me. I don't like being shut out. Answer the question or we have nothing left to talk about."

The truth of Leo's words hit me like a wrecking ball. He was right. I committed the number one relationship sin in Leo's book when I failed the honesty test. I marinated in guilt as I tried to come up with something to say to justify my actions.

Leo prodded me to respond, but I had to honor my end of the bargain with Parker and Santoni. The three of us agreed it was best for Leo if we didn't tell him about the true nature of my gift. For now, I had to stick with the story I revealed publically. Feeling trapped, I shut down. My defense mechanism was silence.

When I failed to answer, it only made him angrier. Leo grabbed his keys and jacket. "Don't wait up for me."

When Leo stormed out the door, my heart dropped to my stomach. My worst-case scenario had come true—I'm on the verge of losing him.

I could never be with a woman who wasn't honest with me.

Trust was the cornerstone of all my relationships. If Evelyn failed to honor the one rule I asked her never to break, then our relationship wouldn't survive. I drove to my favorite dive bar in the old neighborhood to clear my head.

None of my buddies were around, but the usual crowd was there, watching sports and downing longnecks on bucket o' beer night. I ordered a Pabst Blue Ribbon and took a seat at the bar.

I didn't mind being alone tonight. It was a relief to listen to my own thoughts without everyone telling me what I should feel or reminding me of what I should know. I was sick of people looking at me like sad puppies when I forgot all the things I was supposed to remember.

I pulled out my phone and checked my messages. Thankfully, I didn't have any texts from Evelyn. She claimed the reason she couldn't tell me the truth was to protect me. If she believed that, then we never belonged together in the first place.

When you love someone, you don't keep secrets.

What had she done that was so horrible for me to know?

While I had my phone out, I scrolled through pictures taken over the last year. Evelyn on the stage of her gallery in front of one of her paintings. Evelyn posing with a glass of wine and looking smoking hot during one of our date nights. Evelyn wrapped in a blanket on our couch, drawing in her sketchpad.

Evelyn with my family. Evelyn cuddled in my arms with the city skyline in the background. Evelyn making the shape of a heart with her hands. Evelyn wearing my Loyola t-shirt as a dress—wait a minute.

I remembered the scene that had played out while I had lost consciousness after my attack. The woman in my dream was wearing my shirt. She had bruises on her arms and lacerations around her wrists from handcuffs or some sort of bondage.

Was that a memory of Evelyn after she'd been attacked?

As I closed my eyes and struggled to recall the memory, someone put their arm on my back, pulling me out of the moment. I opened my eyes to see who it was—a woman I knew from the past.

A smoking hot lady with a knockout body I'd spent time with under the sheets…before Evelyn.

"Did you and your girlfriend have a fight?" She pointed at the photo of Evelyn I'd been staring at on my phone.

"How's it going, Rochelle?"

My old flame smiled seductively and rested her hand on my thigh. "What are you doing here all alone tonight, Leo?" She slurped down the last of her amaretto sour then slid the cherry into her mouth and sucked out the juice.

She locked her gaze on mine as she pulled the stem out slowly and licked her luscious, full lips. Rochelle set her empty glass on the bar and pushed it toward the bartender.

"I'll take another one, and Leo wants a PBR." She pulled up a barstool and settled in beside me.

This familiar scene felt like I had picked up right where I'd left off. In my scrambled brain, I'd been in Rochelle's bed only a few nights ago. The scent of her perfume, the seductive way she touched me, and hanging out in the bar with a no-strings-attached relationship policy gave me an odd sense of comfort.

Like a bolt of lightning struck me, I realized that the way I'd been living life a year ago seemed a hell of a lot less complicated compared to my new life with Evelyn.

ACTION—EVELYN

*L*eo never came home last night.

I waited up well past three AM, hoping he had just gone out with his buddies to have a beer to calm down.

If that were the case, where did he go after closing time? I figured he had met up with Santoni or Parker and ended up spending the night in one of their spare bedrooms.

The last thing I needed to do was text his friends to track him down. He would be even angrier at me if I dragged his buddies into our fight.

I was too nervous to sleep. When Leo came home, it would be Judgment Day. I should've told him the truth the first time he asked for it. Now I had to do damage control on top of coming clean about my paranormal gift.

In order to prove I was telling the truth, I would have to show him my sketches of the decapitated woman I believed was his missing person—Sloane Matthews.

And I'm the only person who has had contact with her in the last year.

How will Leo handle it when I'm the one who has to tell him that Sloane is dead?

After I dreamed of her, I sketched morbid photos of her crime scene and detailed drawings that would help Leo's team solve her case.

I'd already sent my automatic drawings to Parker and gave him details about my dream. I was glad he had the information as he worked the case, but I hated to keep this vital information from Leo. I wanted to tell him everything, but how could I explain any of this to Leo when he never believed in ghosts or paranormal phenomena?

If I had any shot of turning my once-again skeptical detective into a believer, I needed more evidence about the case. In order to do that, I had to go straight to the source—Sloane Matthews.

It was now four o'clock in the morning.

Leo wasn't coming home.

Instead of sitting here and worrying, I needed to take action. So, I broke another one of Detective Ricci's rules—I left the apartment without informing him where I was going.

INVITATION—EVELYN

The gallery was eerily quiet this time of night.

My painted ghosts peeked at me through the darkness as I moved through the empty building. As I climbed the stairs to reach my studio, the tapping of my shoes on the wooden stairs echoed across the hallway.

I slid my key into the lock and entered my sacred space. The familiar scent of wet paint and turpentine welcomed my artistic soul back to my creative kingdom.

I dimmed the lights and turned on my salt lamps to energize my space. I cranked up a Fleetwood Mac playlist and grooved along with "The Chain" as I squirted paint on my palette and set out my supplies.

The moment I touched my brushes and placed a blank canvas onto my easel, my mind, body, and spirit lifted. When I left our apartment, the sting of old wounds seeped open and brought back the pain of feeling unloved from my past.

The aftermath of my gift had caused me to be estranged from my parents after the accident. I reasoned that was why I lied to Leo—my fear of being alone and unloved.

Concentrate on the one thing no one can take away—your art.

I had a life outside of Leo, and I needed to find the strength to hold it together as our relationship weathered what I deeply hoped would be just a passing storm. Leo didn't leave me, he was just angry and needed some space.

Then why hadn't he come home?

As I stared at the blank canvas, I rolled a wide brush into red, blue, and green paint with a dash of yellow to make a burnt umber color. Then I dabbed in some mars black, a touch of emerald green, and marked my canvas with long, loose swipes of rich, earthy tones to set the mood for the undertones.

In the middle of the night, there were no rules. I wasn't working for a client or because I had a deadline for an upcoming show. I closed my eyes and mentally called out to the universe to guide me along my artistic journey.

I opened my third eye, held my brush in hand, and allowed my muse to take over.

Lead me where I need to go… help me find you, Sloane.

As my hand moved across the canvas, the sensation of hot breath on my neck stirred me out of my meditative state. A low growl rumbled behind me, inching closer and closer to my neck.

The odor of musky fur and foul breath filled the air as a predatory animal came within striking range. My blood ran cold as a human-sized red wolf circled me and snarled as I stood before my canvas, frozen with fear.

Run, Evelyn!

While my instincts urged me to flee, I knew it was impossible to outrun the beast. I slid my hand down and searched for a weapon to use against the massive animal. My hand bumped into a long wooden handle.

I glanced down and found—an axe.

I lifted the heavy tool with both hands and held it level to my chest. The wolf lowered his head and bared his teeth, daring me to take a swing at him. If I lifted the blade above my head, he would strike before I could take a swing.

The door that led to the main gallery was close enough for me to make a run for it before the animal reached me. My odds of running seemed only slightly the more survivable option.

Once I decided to go, I couldn't waver.

One…two…three…

I bolted for the door.

The chase was on.

I reached the doorway and escaped before the wolf caught me, but when I tried to shut him out, the wolf was already halfway through.

I screamed as I fled down the stairs with the wolf hot on my tail. When I reached the landing, I ran into the pitch-black darkness of my ghostly gallery. But instead of seeing my paintings of the dead and my dark angels on the walls, I found myself alone in a forest.

I searched the trees for the wolf, but he was hiding somewhere in the shadows.

"Evelyn!" Leo's deep voice echoed through the forest.

"I'm here, Leo. Where are you?' As I ran toward the sound of Leo's voice, the wolf jumped on the trail ahead and prowled toward me. When I turned to run in the opposite direction, a second, bushy black wolf had crept up on me, blocking my escape.

The red wolf went for my throat and knocked me flat on my back. While I was down, the other one joined the attack, tearing and ripping at my flesh. I writhed and kicked and fought them with all the strength I had, but without Leo, I could never fight them off.

"No! Leave me alone. Help me, Leo!"

A loud buzz woke me from my nightmare.

When I opened my eyes, a single word popped into my head—Aurora.

The same clairaudient message I received after I dreamed of Sloane.

I panted as I came down from my nightmare. The dream was so vivid and terrifying, it was hard to catch my breath.

As I forced myself to breathe, I stared at the now-finished painting I had started before the dream.

Holy crap. I stared into the haunting dark eyes of a tall, ghostly woman. Her long dress was buttoned up to her neck, and her leather lace-up boots reminded me of the late 1930's fashion. While her stern expression and post-mortem decay were jarring, the most haunting aspect of the painting was in the background.

The restless spirit pointed a bony finger at a small cemetery set deep in the woods. A cluster of small graves stood beneath a tree. With the moonlight casting down on the granite markers, I could make out the dates on the memorials, but not the names.

All the graves belonged to young children who had passed nearly a hundred years ago. The woman may have been showing me where her children were buried. As I studied my art, I wondered what this painting had to do with the wolves in my dream.

My cell had been buzzing since I opened my eyes.

Answer it, Evelyn. It could be Leo.

I stumbled over to my drafting table and grabbed my phone.

My eyes widened when I checked the name on the screen —Dr. Vaughn Reynolds.

"Hello?"

"Evelyn, so good to hear your voice. How are you?" He sounded stressed, although his tone was light.

"Dr. Vaughn. What a surprise. I'm okay. What's going on?"

Why is he calling me before dawn?

He was silent for a moment as he processed my response. "I have an important matter to discuss with you. Something unusual has been happening, and you're the only person who might understand what I'm experiencing. I'm hoping you will come for a visit. Bridgemont is beautiful this time of year."

His invitation shocked me. We had lost touch, and I hadn't spoken to him for months. Not since he left town after a serial killer murdered his wife.

What is so important that Vaughn needs to discuss in person?

HOME—LEO

I stayed the night at Santoni's place.

He had come into the bar just after Rochelle and I started talking about old times. I used to go back to her place at closing time and spend the evening with the sexy Italian bombshell under her satin sheets.

In my mind, I was still that carefree bachelor.

I liked my no-strings-attached lifestyle that I remembered, but I was a loyal guy and would never cheat on Evelyn —but the temptation was right there, wearing skin-tight jeans and a low-cut blouse.

Which was why my buddy Santoni was quick to offer me a place to stay for the night.

"Rise and shine, Leo." In the morning, Santoni stepped out of his bedroom and hovered over the couch where I'd slept. "Hurry up and get ready. I want to show you something today."

"What?"

"It's a surprise."

"You know, I'm getting fed up with all the fucking surprises lately."

"This is a good one. Trust me."

The word trust was grating on my nerves, too.

Every day since my attack had been a new adventure, and today was no exception. I was grateful my buddy wasn't grilling me about not going home to Evelyn last night. He knew me well enough to know I didn't want to talk about my domestic problems or how I was handling the emotional stress of my memory loss.

When Santoni and I hit the road, we reminisced about growing up in our old neighborhood. I was glad to get a break from all the drama that had become my life and relieved to kick back and feel like my old self again as we headed out of the city toward the suburbs.

After about a thirty-minute drive, Santoni pulled down a street in a transitional neighborhood. There was a mix of older homes, tear-downs, and handyman specials with for-sale signs in the yard.

Santoni rolled up to a fixer-upper with a "Sold" sign in the yard.

"What are we doing here?"

He grinned without answering me as we got out of the car. I followed him curiously down the sidewalk that led to the backyard.

The house was a work in progress, with most of the renovations already completed. Fresh green grass, tidy bushes, and pavers led the way to an outdoor grill and a couple of picnic tables.

A tall privacy fence ran the length of the property, making this space a complete outdoor oasis. While someone's hard work on the renovations impressed me, I didn't understand why Santoni had brought me here. "What are you, a realtor now?"

"Welcome home, Leo. This place is all yours."

I gave him a skeptical glare. "What are you talking about? I don't own a home."

"When you sold your old place, you started looking for a new one. You're only renting the apartment until you finish the renovations. This is the dream home you remodeled for you and Evelyn."

I stared in shock as I scanned the house. Fresh paint, new shutters, covered porch...

"Check out the inside. We've been working on this place behind Evelyn's back for months."

I followed Santoni up the back stairs. He entered a code on the lockbox and retrieved the key. Inside, the house was clean, but there were still some renovations left to do.

On the counter, there was a box with a big red bow on top loaded with color swatches and design samples. Next to that, there was a bouquet of flowers and a card with Evelyn's name scrolled across the center.

"Leo, I know this is hard for you, but I couldn't wait any longer before telling you about what almost happened."

My gut was in knots as the big picture was coming into focus.

"On the day of the attack, you were supposed to be here. You had a whole day planned for Evelyn, and you were going to bring her here to surprise her."

As the realization hit me that Santoni was not yanking my chain, my range of emotions went from shock to excitement to dread. "Evelyn doesn't know about this place yet?"

"No."

"Does my family know?"

Santoni scratched the back of his neck. "You need to talk to your mom about that."

I had gone to a lot of trouble to surprise the woman I loved. The woman I had walked out on last night—the same woman who didn't trust me enough to tell me the truth.

Maybe I lost my memory for a reason. What if this was never supposed to happen? Evelyn and I had not yet taken the next step in our relationship, and maybe that was for the best.

If we never got back together, I would have a place of my own, and she could start fresh wherever she chose. We could split up without a big financial hassle and go our separate ways without a lot of drama.

I took one more look around the yard. "I could fit my entire family back here. What did I have planned on the day of the attack?"

"Go talk to your mom. You planned everything with her. Silvia loves Evelyn as much as you do. She'd walk through fire to help you find your way back to her."

Damn. So much for an easy breakup.

WHEN WE GOT BACK to Santoni's place, I had a voluptuous surprise leaning against my car, holding a plate of sandwiches covered in plastic wrap.

"No fucking way," Santoni said. "She's got nerve."

"Why do you say that?" I asked.

Santoni shot me an incredulous stare. "Because you're with Evelyn. Rochelle has no business hanging around you, bringing you sandwiches."

"I'll see what she wants."

Rochelle waved as we pulled into the driveway and headed my way.

"I know what she wants, dumbass—you. She's been hot for you for years," Santoni snapped. "She's nothing but trouble, Leo. Don't play into her trap. If I were you, I'd tell her to get lost."

"Thanks for the advice," I said sarcastically.

Rochelle's hips swayed as she approached. "Hey, Leo. I got

a favor to ask you. My car broke down and I need a ride downtown. Do you think you could drop me off on your way home?" A sinful smile curled up on her lips.

The right thing to do was follow my buddy's advice and tell her to get lost. Evelyn and I were still a couple, and I wasn't going to jump back into bed with my old flame just because I had a fight with my girlfriend.

But I was fed up with everyone telling me what to do and how to think and who to love. It wasn't a crime to give someone a lift downtown, and I was tired of living by everyone else's rules.

"Sure. Get in. I'll drop you off."

BUSTED—EVELYN

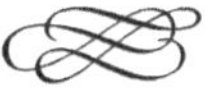

My energy was zapped from painting all night.

I needed some fresh air and walked home from the gallery on the warm and breezy fall morning. The seasonal clock had rung the Spooky Season bell, and the neighborhood shops were dressed up and decorated in all their fall finery.

Grinning Jack-o'-lanterns, black cats with witchy hats, and ghostly ghouls haunted the storefronts as I strolled down the sidewalk, thinking about Leo. He hadn't contacted me since he stormed out last night.

Could I blame him? I'd let my fear of losing him cloud my judgment. He deserved to know the truth. I held my phone in hand in case he called. The street was lightly populated in the mid-morning hour, and I wondered if Leo would be home when I got there.

Is he ready to talk?

How will he react when he sees me?

Leo and I have had our share of disagreements over the past year. He's a high-octane guy and not shy about speaking his mind. I was passive by nature and let things go more easily than he did. My domestic style was to avoid confrontation. Leo took a head-on approach and tackled issues in real-time.

When I reached our apartment, I opened the door and called Leo's name.

No answer.

I tossed my purse on the couch and scooped Duke's food into his bowl. While the dog was eating, I checked the spare bedroom in case Leo was resting. I reasoned he might've been sleeping and hadn't heard me come in.

The room was empty.

Is he going to avoid me forever?

I went into the bathroom and splashed cold water on my face. As I patted my skin dry, I studied my reflection in the mirror. I was exhausted, and the physical effects of stress were clear on my face.

Pull yourself together, Evelyn.

I took the dog out for a quick walk, then rounded up my laptop and all the sketches I'd drawn since Leo's attack. I set up a workstation in the living room and scooted aside the candles and books on the coffee table to make room for my drawings.

I fired up my laptop and typed Sloane's name into the search engine. I scanned the news headlines about her disappearance, read social media posts, and scrolled through crime blogs about her case.

From everything I'd read, it seemed Sloane was a well-loved, outgoing college student who had vanished from a Halloween party. On the night of her disappearance, she was last seen wearing a Little Red Riding Hood costume.

The same outfit she was wearing in my dream.

I jotted down notes and then searched for information about the prime suspect in the case—Professor Nolan Bradford. Headlines torched him for having an affair with his student, and there were pages and pages of bloggers making nasty allegations about his involvement in her disappearance.

While I researched the case, I spread out my sketches and tried to connect the drawings to specific events related to the crime. If Sloane was Little Red on the night of the party, who was the Big Bad Wolf?

As I worked, I let out a series of yawns and needed to take a break. I snapped pictures of my drawings and sent them to Parker, along with details of my latest dream.

When Parker didn't immediately get back to me, I laid down on the couch to rest my eyes, but exhaustion got the better of me, and I drifted off to sleep.

"Evelyn." Someone tapped me on the arm and woke me from my nap.

I opened my eyes and found Leo beside me.

"Leo…How are you?"

He didn't answer because he was distracted by my crime scene sketches spread out on our coffee table. A rush of panic jolted me upright when I realized I had carelessly left my automatic drawings in plain sight.

"Leo, please don't be mad. There's a reason why—"

At that moment, my phone pinged with incoming texts from Parker. My screen was locked, so the messages were not visible, but his name popped up on the screen in rapid-fire succession.

Leo didn't need to be a detective to process my crime scene. From his vantage point, I had drawn his missing person—Sloane Matthews—as an animated corpse. There was no reasonable explanation in his mind other than I was making a mockery of the victim and his investigation.

"Evelyn, I'm speechless. I don't even know what to say right now."

"I'm so sorry, Leo. I swear I'm not trying to hurt you—"

"You keep saying that, but what else am I supposed to make of this? And you're sending these drawings to my partner?" He pointed at my phone. "You need to tell me what's going on."

I had no choice. Leo needed to know the truth. "I'm a medium, Leo. I can communicate with the dead. Your missing person, Sloane Matthews, has been communicating with me from beyond the grave. I'm sorry to tell you…she is no longer alive."

Leo glared at me as my confession seeped under his skin. "Don't fuck with me right now, Evelyn."

"This is the truth I didn't want to tell you, Leo. Ghosts visit me in my dreams, and they communicate with me through my art. I told you about that part at my gallery. But what I didn't tell you is what they convey to me. They want my help. Sometimes they show me how they died or point to evidence about the crime. Sloane came to me in a dream…"

As I spilled my secrets, I watched Leo's respect for me dissolve before my eyes. "We have a problem, Evelyn. Like I told you at the gallery, I don't believe in ghosts. Whatever this is—whatever you think you're doing—I don't like it."

Leo raked his hands through his hair as he reached the tipping point of our argument. I wasn't a fighter, but Leo wouldn't stop questioning me until he got a confession out of me. "What does this have to do with snake eyes? How did you know about that?"

"I don't know what it means. It was just a phrase that popped into my head at the restaurant. It's called a clairaudient message—a word or phrase that comes to me from the spirit world." I tried to come up with something to help him understand, but—

Someone knocked on our apartment door.

Leo's eyes widened. His expression morphed from anger to guilt.

"Who is that?" I asked.

"Evelyn, it's not what you think. Stay here. I'll go take care of it."

I hopped off the couch and trailed behind Leo as he headed toward the door. But before I could open it, a woman I recognized from Leo's past opened the door and walked into our home as if she belonged there.

"Hey, Leo. I need to pee. Can I—" Rochelle stopped mid-sentence when she realized I was home and had busted up their afternoon hook-up.

That explained where my boyfriend slept last night.

CRUMBLED—EVELYN

The sight of Rochelle hovering by my man in her skin-tight jeans and a sleazy blouse launched daggers from my eyes.

"Hey, Evelyn. Leo and I were just—"

"You need to leave, Rochelle," Leo said.

"But I need a ride downtown, Leo. We can have lunch on the way. I've got the sandwiches right here," Rochelle fired back with a sultry smile as she tried to convince Leo she was the better choice.

I shifted my gaze between them, floored by Leo's betrayal and pissed beyond belief that Rochelle was trying to muscle in on my man. I knew about their romantic fling before Leo and I started dating, but according to him, the relationship had been strictly physical. Who was I to expect a man wouldn't have his past romances?

But running back to her bed the second we had a fight. Seriously?

When Rochelle didn't budge from our living room, I clenched my fists and fought the urge to shove her out of our living room by force. I had never felt threatened by another woman, but knowing Leo craved her body and the cheap scent of her come fuck me drugstore perfume, I worried he might choose the less-complicated option over the weirdo artist who had magically materialized in his bed.

"Take an Uber, Rochelle. I need to talk to Evelyn."

"What about the sandwiches? Rochelle lifted the plate and tossed Leo a pouty expression. But when Leo didn't respond, she took the hint that she wasn't welcome in our home. "Fine. I'll catch up with you later."

Leo closed the door behind her, then turned to face me. But before he could spin a bullshit story of why he was hanging out with his ex-lover, I fired first. "Did you sleep with her last night?"

"No."

"Did you call her after our fight?"

"I went to the bar. She was there. That's it."

"If you saw her last night, why are you with her today?" I crossed my arms and held my breath. Never once during our relationship had I ever worried about Leo hooking up when he went to the bar, but this situation had cheater slashed all over it.

His job was demanding, and he worked long hours day and night. I never asked him where he was or what he was doing because we trusted each other. But catching him red-handed with her—what was I supposed to think?

The image of Leo and Rochelle together gutted me to the point I felt like I might pass out. How did our relationship go from paradise to the gutter in a matter of days?

"I said I didn't sleep with her. That's all you need to know." Leo lifted his chin indignantly.

"Why are you with her? Why did you bring her back to our apartment when my car wasn't parked out front? I left it at the gallery, but you thought I wasn't home, right? Tell me the truth, Leo. I need to trust—"

"Trust? You have nerve, Evelyn. What about when I asked you to tell me the truth? And as for your ghost story, I don't believe a word of it." Leo's tone had risen to a nuclear level.

Tears streamed down my cheeks as the sting of his accusation pierced my heart. Duke trotted to my side and leaned against my leg as if his mission was to absorb my pain.

I stood silent and let Leo vent his frustrations and take out his anger on me. He ranted about how he couldn't be in a relationship with someone who couldn't be honest with him.

"I'm a detective, Evelyn. You know I have ways of uncovering the truth. Whatever you're not telling me, I'll find out with or without your help."

I stood there stunned as Leo went on, berating me and justifying why he didn't need to explain his actions last night. His words stung, but the more animated he became, the more I tuned out his hurtful accusations.

This wasn't like Leo at all. None of this was—not his storming out last night, not tearing me down, not calling me a liar. The man standing before me, ranting, was a guy who was used to being in charge, now feeling utterly out of control because of his memory loss.

"Are you going to say anything, Evelyn?"

What? I focused back in and shook my head. "I'm listening."

Leo raked his hand through his hair and paced the room. After a few deep breaths and a moment of silence, Leo's anger seemed to simmer down to a low boil.

"I'm sorry I yelled. I had no right to take my anger out on you."

"This isn't you, Leo. You don't talk to me this way. I'm sorry for my part in this, truly. But this isn't your normal behavior."

"In my head, I'm still the guy who never wanted a committed relationship. My job is the most important part of my life, and I hate sitting on the sidelines while the perp who attacked me is still out there." He seemed to decompress. His voice was settling into a neutral tone.

"I understand completely. Hopefully, your memory will return soon, and things will go back to normal."

Leo clenched his jaw as he considered his response. "That's the dilemma I'm facing now, Evelyn. What if I don't want things to go back to normal? What if I liked my life the way it was before? A life with no strings attached."

My blood ran cold when I realized where Leo's thoughts were headed.

"It seems to me, my life was a hell of a lot better—" Leo bit his tongue, unwilling to finish his sentence.

But I understood his message and finished his thoughts for him. "Your life was a hell of a lot better—before you met me."

"I never said that." Leo stared at the ceiling as he tried to calm down. "I can't have this conversation right now, Evelyn. I'm going to stay at Santoni's for a couple of days and work some things out."

I forced myself to breathe so I wouldn't pass out. "No. This is your place. I'll leave. I'll stay at my studio."

Without waiting for a response, I leaned down and said goodbye to Duke. "I love you, sweet boy. If I don't see you again, have a great retirement."

I grabbed my purse, and as I headed out the door, I had an overwhelming urge to say one more thing. I had absolutely nothing to lose at this point, and dropping another paranormal bombshell on him wouldn't make a difference. "The evidence is in the safe."

"What evidence? What are you talking about?" Leo asked.

I pointed to my head to reference the source of the

clairaudient message. "You're the detective. I'm sure you'll have no problem figuring it out."

"You're right. I will figure it out, Evelyn," he said. "And just so we're clear, I don't want you involved in my investigations, and I don't want you to contact my partner again. Do you understand?"

I gave Leo a nod as I left our apartment. When the door closed behind me, my world crumbled. As I walked away from the man I loved, the reality set in that Leo no longer wanted to be a part of my strange and fucked-up life.

In my heart, I always knew one day my gift would cost me everything, and now that truth had come to fruition.

This was the beginning of the end of us.

HIDDEN—LEO

When Evelyn left, my gut told me our relationship was over.

Couples fight. Everyone in a committed relationship argues now and then. Evelyn had a right to be angry that I was hanging around with Rochelle, and I had a right to call her out for not being honest with me.

But I really laid into her.

Shit. I had no right to yell at her and cut her down the way I had. Evelyn was a gentle soul, and I let my frustrations get the better of me.

If my mother or one of my four sisters heard those vile words come out of my mouth, they would've attacked me like a pride of she-lions and taken me down by the throat.

And why the fuck was I hanging around with Rochelle?

If Evelyn had brought an ex-lover into our home, I would've lost my mind. But instead of owning my mistake, I blamed her for all my problems and kicked her out of our home.

What kind of man have I become?

My life was spinning out of control, and I needed to face my problems and get a hold of myself.

I sank down on the couch to cool off before I called Evelyn to apologize. While I mentally kicked myself in the ass, my gaze landed on Evelyn's morbid sketches on the coffee table.

I leaned in for a closer look. The first one was a drawing of my missing person, Sloane Matthews—but apparently, she was no longer among the living.

Fucking hell.

The artist sketched her body laid out on the ground over a pile of leaves. The corpse had blood splatter on her Halloween costume and there was a fucking axe buried in her chest.

Sloane's eyes were wide open with shock and her expression was frozen in a manner that suggested she screamed her last breath. I recognized the victim and the location where she was last seen—those two pieces of information were facts in my case.

But since we had never recovered a body, Sloane's fate was still unknown. I picked up the drawing and inspected the fine details. At the bottom of the page, Evelyn had written a series of numbers.

I tore a fresh sheet of paper from her sketchbook and wrote them down. Then I picked up the next sketch—a bunch of creepy old Victorian dolls. Instead of numbers, there was a word scrolled across the bottom of the page.

Aurora.

The next drawing featured a bonfire with melting body parts. Damn. Evelyn sure had a wicked imagination. This one went back to a number sequence: 11-19-52.

What the hell?

These weren't numbers, it was a date. Specifically, my grandmother's birthday. What kind of game was Evelyn playing? Wait a minute...I'd used these numbers before as a six-digit password.

"The evidence is in the safe."

I rushed to my office and entered the numbers on the safe's digital lock.

Click! The safe opened. Inside, I found a stack of case files, a set of my new house keys, and an envelope with the word "Confidential" stamped across the center in red ink.

I opened the envelope and found pages and pages of Evelyn's sketches from my past cases. In my line of work, I had become accustomed to gruesome images and macabre crime-scene photos. Evelyn's drawings were disturbing, graphic, and hauntingly accurate.

Among my files, I came across crime scene photos from the Sloane Matthews investigation. There was no body, but we found blood, a patent leather shoe, and an article of torn clothing from the costume Little Red Riding Hood Sloane was last seen wearing.

Is this the evidence Evelyn wanted me to find?

I grabbed a magnifying glass from my drawer and studied the fine details of Evelyn's sketches. There, drawn in the bonfire flames, was the evidence we had recovered from the scene of Sloane's last known location, hidden in Evelyn's pictures.

A blotchy shadow in the bloodstain's shape.

The patent leather shoe tucked next to a log.

The checked fabric of the dress disguised in the shape of a flame.

I had never released the photos of my crime scenes to the public. The only way Evelyn would have access to this information was—if she had been telling me the truth about her gift.

OLD WOUNDS—EVELYN

$\mathcal{M}$y life was a hell of a lot better...before I met you.

Leo may not have said those exact words, but his sentiment weighed down my soul like a cinder block wrapped around my heart. I dragged my body back to my gallery and holed up in my studio to process the downward spiral that had become my life.

While my first reaction was to curl up in a ball and hide from the world, Leo and I were facing a relationship crisis, and I needed to figure out a solution for our mounting problems.

This was a recipe for making things worse, not better. I had to find a way to convince him I was telling the truth. I tried to stay positive as I came up with a plan, but I couldn't shake Leo's harsh assessment of our relationship.

My life was a hell of a lot better...before I met you.

I thought about how our relationship evolved after my friend went missing, and I had tangled myself up in his investigation. Thinking about that time opened up old wounds we had suffered when my gift seeped into our world more than once and had nearly cost us our lives.

My gift was dangerous. Communicating with the dead was risky business. I've known this since the beginning. As I tried to convince myself that Leo was wrong about his harsh assessment of our relationship, all the evidence pointed right back to what he had said in the heat of the moment.

His life would be a hell of a lot better without me in it.

My cell phone buzzed, waking me from a deep sleep.

I had gone over my case files until the early morning hour and crashed on the couch after reading up on paranormal phenomena.

I grabbed my phone and tapped the screen. "Hey, Mom. How's it going?"

"Good morning, Leo. I hope I didn't wake you." We talked about how I was feeling and if I needed anything, but she sounded worried about something.

"What's wrong?"

"Is Evelyn with you? I've been trying to reach her since last night, but she hasn't called me back."

I checked my watch. I'd slept in later than I'd thought. "No. She's not here. She's probably working and has her phone off. Do you need something?"

Mom was silent a moment before she answered. "It's not like Evelyn not to get back to me. We were planning on having lunch today. Did she say anything about that?"

I wouldn't know because I hadn't spoken to her since I'd effectively crushed her soul.

Fucking hell, Ricci.

Evelyn had left the apartment yesterday afternoon. She took her purse with her, and I reasoned she had her phone, too. I opened an app to check the location of her cell. The red dot pinpointed her location—Halsted. Evelyn was at her gallery—at least, her phone was there.

"She's at work, Mom. She must've forgotten about lunch. If I see her, I'll tell her to call you."

"Aren't you worried?" Mom asked.

"Why would I be?"

"Because she's not returning my calls," Mom snapped. "We need to find out where she is. Have you spoken to her?"

"Not since yesterday. If it will make you feel better—"

"Yesterday?" Mom squawked. "Where did you sleep last night?"

"Mom, calm down. I'm sure Evelyn is—"

"What happened? Did you two have a fight?"

Coming from a big family, it was impossible to keep my loved ones out of my business. I grew up with four sisters. There was no such thing as privacy in our home. To this day, my family is very close. Which was a blessing—except when I didn't want my personal life examined under a microscope.

Mom continued to questioned me about why we weren't together and why I wasn't concerned that Evelyn was not answering her phone. I tried to calm her down and told her I didn't want my family interfering in my private life, but my sharp tongue brought her to tears.

"You need to come over. Now. I have something that belongs to you," Mom said.

"What is it? Can it wait?"

"No. You had something important on you when you

were admitted into the hospital. When I got there, the staff gave it to me for safekeeping. I need to give it back to you."

"Just tell me what it is."

Mom let out a sympathetic sigh. "I know you're having a hard time, son. Please come over. I'm worried about you, too."

Mom guilt was the most powerful weapon known to humankind. "I'll swing by the gallery first, then I'll be over."

"Thank you, sweetie. See you soon."

As I left the apartment, I had a bad feeling Mom was right —I needed to check on Evelyn.

When I got to Halsted Street, the lights were off at Evelyn's place.

I didn't know if her gallery was supposed to be open this time of day or not, but there was an event schedule in the window and a sign that read, "Gallery hours by appointment only."

Evelyn's studio was on the third floor and inaccessible from the street. Since she wasn't answering my calls, I used the security app on my phone to gain access to the building.

When I got inside, I scanned the room for signs of life. It appeared no one was around on the first floor. As I climbed the steps to Evelyn's studio, I studied her framed sketches along the wall.

There was a woman dressed in a nurse's uniform holding a little dog. The drawing was sketched with photographic accuracy. I couldn't say for sure, but I reasoned that was Evelyn's drawing of the "angel" that stayed by her side at the hospital after her near-fatal accident.

I obviously checked into the details of her report, beginning with the 9-1-1 call her friend made when she feared

Evelyn had drowned. Everything Evelyn had told me about her accident and the events that followed all checked out.

At least I knew she was telling me the truth about that part of her life—and death.

When I reached her studio, I knocked on the door.

No answer.

After a few moments, I knocked again.

I knew she was there because I tracked her phone to this location and her car was out front.

It occurred to me that maybe she wasn't ready to talk. Too bad. I was worried about her and needed to confirm she was safe "Evelyn, it's me. Can you let me in?"

I stood still and listened for signs of life behind the door. The only noise came from the city life on the street and some soft music from inside her studio. I was about to knock again, but stopped when a shadow spilled out from under the door.

I waited for Evelyn to let me in, but she hesitated, as if deciding on whether or not she was ready to face me.

Guilt flooded over me, knowing how badly I had hurt her. I was angry about my situation, confused about all the paranormal crap, and frustrated that I couldn't remember my life.

Through it all, Evelyn had been patient and stood by me —until now.

"Evelyn," I said softly. "You have every right to be angry with me. I treated you horribly, and I'm sorry."

I paused to let the apology sink in, but Evelyn still wouldn't open the door.

Considering I had a list of offenses I was guilty of, I figured I would cover them all, hoping I could convince her to let me in.

"Nothing happened between me and Rochelle. I spent the night at Santoni's place. Rochelle saw me in the morning and asked me to give her a ride downtown. I didn't know if you were home or not, so I stopped by before I dropped her off to check on Duke. No other reason."

I pressed my hand on the door and waited for a response that never came.

The last thing I said before I walked away was, "I'm sorry I hurt you, Evelyn."

GOODBYE—EVELYN

’m sorry I hurt you, too, Leo. I placed my hand on the door and sobbed silently until the sound of his footsteps echoed down the stairs.

The truth of his words were engraved on my heart like a battle wound. I wanted to let him in, but I couldn’t face him. The pain stemming from our argument had kept me up all night. I’d lost my appetite and hadn’t eaten since yesterday morning.

I needed to pull myself together and fix things, but even the strong and brave woman I had become over the last year needed time to recover from that soul-crushing gut-punch of an argument.

I would never give up on us. I loved Leo with all my heart. For now, though, we both needed some time and space apart to recover from our fight. Dr. Vaughn was expecting me later today. My bags were packed, and I was ready to go.

I told him I would let him know when I hit the road. I had some work to take care of at the gallery before I left town. Bridgemont was about three hours away, and I would make it to his place before dark.

I waited a few minutes to make sure Leo had left the gallery before I moved to the window to search for his car. There was no sign of him, so I could leave whenever I was ready.

Vaughn's message was cryptic, but I was curious why he had called me out of the blue and wanted to see me. We'd bonded over our shared experience with a serial killer last fall, and even Leo and Vaughn had become friendly, which seemed impossible considering their past.

But Leo remembers nothing about that.

Enough. Stop blaming Leo for his memory loss.

I second-guessed my silence moments ago. While Leo was apologizing to my door, I should've let him in and told him how sorry I was for keeping my secret. I was given an impossible choice, and if I had the chance to do it over, I would've handled it differently.

I don't know if that would've made things better, but hearing him accuse me of lying last night had hit me harder than any of this. Prior to his assault, Leo and I trusted each other completely.

I never wanted to lie to him, but when faced with the decision, it seemed the truth would've hurt him more—because he would've thought I was nuts. I dabbed a tissue under my eyes, took a deep cleansing breath, and turned off all the lights.

As I rolled my suitcase to the door, I glanced around my studio and smiled as if I were saying goodbye to an old friend. I was only going to be gone for a couple of days to give Leo some space, but I was already feeling homesick as I slid on my shades, locked up the gallery, and headed down the sidewalk.

Just ahead, I spotted a cool and handsome brick wall of a man leaning against my Audi. Leo had been staking out my gallery, waiting for me to resurface. I thought he had left after I refused to let him into my studio, but Leo wasn't the kind of guy who gave up easily.

Even though I was mad at him, Leo looked hot in his dark jeans, a muscle-hugging t-shirt, and a black leather jacket. My first instinct was to run to him and wrap my arms around him. I hated how we left things, but he was the one who asked for a break, and the last thing I would do was come sniveling back to him.

I straightened my shoulders and faced my ripped and toned obstacle with a confident strut. "Good afternoon, Leo. What a surprise to see you here," I said sarcastically.

"Hey, Evelyn. I was just passing by. Glad I caught you." Leo took the suitcase from my hand. "Let me help you with your bag. Going somewhere nice?"

So this was the game he wanted to play? "I don't know. I hope so."

I popped the trunk, and Leo loaded my bag.

"Where are you headed?"

There were two reasons I didn't want to tell Leo where I was going. The first was the most obvious—he would be jealous I was going to visit another man.

Dr. Vaughn was a handsome heart surgeon who had recently become a widower. He and I were friends, nothing else, but since he had flaunted his ex in front of me, I didn't want him to consider my visit as a means of retaliation.

Second, Dr. Vaughn and I had something in common that Leo would find unsettling. We both had near-death experiences. I never spoke to Vaughn about my gift, but my sixth sense was telling me his request to see me was related to something he was having a hard time coming to grips with—same as me when I had come back from the dead.

Plus, I was still licking my wounds from our last argument. I wasn't mentally prepared for another fight, and anything I said at this point might set him off.

"I'm going to Bridgemont to visit a friend for a few days." No matter what, I would never lie to Leo again. Even if the truth hurt him.

"Bridgemont, Indiana? That's off the grid. Who do you know way out there?"

"Just a friend who moved away a few months ago. We'd been planning on meeting up, and I finally have the time now." I stood by the door of my car, but Leo was blocking me and wouldn't move.

"Anyone I know?"

"Yes."

Leo lifted his eyebrows when he sensed I was being evasive. Aggressively so. "What's the address in case I need to reach you?"

"This feels like an interrogation, Leo. If I remember correctly, you are the one who wanted time away from me."

Leo dropped the tough guy façade and tugged on my arm. "Evelyn, I'm sorry. Please don't go."

My instincts urged me to stay. I didn't want to spend time away from Leo, and the idea of going home and working things out seemed like the perfect solution to solving our problems.

But words weren't enough. We were both hurt and angry after our fight and needed space. A road trip to a new place to spend time with my platonic friend was something I would've never done without Leo.

I needed a few days of freedom, and Leo would have to accept my decision.

Leo tapped his foot against my front tire. "You know, the tire pressure looks low. Want me to go with you and fill it up with some air?"

"I have some things to do at work before I leave. I'll take care of it before I hit the road." I wrapped my finger around his belt loop and drew him to me. "I love you. We'll work things out when I get home. I'll be back in a couple of days."

I kissed him softly on the lips, then coaxed him out of my way. He stood beside the door as I buckled into the driver's seat. "Goodbye, Leo."

CONSEQUENCES—LEO

I picked up the dog and headed out to the new house to clear my head. Whatever Mom had to give me could wait.

All I could think about was Evelyn. Our problems. Our past. Our future. I needed to take a mental break from work and my screwed-up life. It was my idea to separate from her for a few days, so why did saying goodbye feel like the biggest mistake of my life?

Focus on something else for a while.

When I got to the house, I set Duke free in the backyard and tossed him the tennis ball. "Search!" Seeing him happily playing fetch without a care in the world helped me relax and reconcile all my mixed feelings.

The doctor said my memory might return in a couple of days, a week, a month, or never. I had to face the harsh reality that I might never remember my past.

Then focus on the present, Ricci.

Whether Evelyn and I survived as a couple remained to be seen. This house, however, was a done deal. I loved fixing things, and while I was off duty and Evelyn was off to Bridgemont, I could get a lot of work done.

I surveyed the construction project in the kitchen. The cabinets needed to be stripped and painted, the light fixtures and appliances had to be replaced, and the old brown tile countertops had to go.

I rifled through the "surprise" box on the counter and figured I had wanted Evelyn to have a hand in the finishing touches of the design.

How thoughtful of me.

All the design shows had modern kitchens with tile back-splashes and fresh countertops. I could've easily just picked out something and finished it before I brought Evelyn here. Unless my artsy girlfriend wanted to do something more her style and finish the kitchen in all black.

I laughed to myself, but part of me wondered if maybe she would opt for a dark and dramatic home setting to match her spooky girl vibe.

I pictured Evelyn loading the house up with her candle collection and hanging drapes that featured her one-of-a-kind spooky designs like the ones she designed on her scarves. I could see her finding hidden gems at thrift stores and picking out cool antique furniture from yard sales.

Evelyn would decorate every inch of this space in a unique way that would showcase her talent and solidify her reputation as the coolest artist in the Windy City. As for me, I didn't care about stuff for the house.

I cared about the people in it.

I stood on the back porch, tossed the ball to the dog, and pictured my life going forward…

My nieces and nephews playing chase in the yard. Mom fussing around the food, making sure everyone had a plate. Santoni making everyone laugh as he told his old stories about growing up in the neighborhood.

As I pictured the scene, I pondered the burning question:

If I never get my memory back, do I want to start over again with Evelyn?

I thought about the sexy and self-assured woman who had rescued me from the hospital and treated me like the most important person in her life. She had been there for me without a flicker of hesitation, a quality I admired about her.

Her artistic talent was unbelievable, and her sexy painting of us was the hottest thing I had ever seen. She was smart, gorgeous, talented, and determined to do everything in her power to help me through my trauma.

Evelyn was every man's dream girl—except for her ghosts.

Was I willing to risk my reputation as a law-enforcement officer, cast aside my own belief system, and trust a woman who claimed she could help me solve my murder investigations by communicating with the ghosts of my victims?

Christ. The thought of me trying to shovel that bullshit story to my team made me sick to my stomach. It was an honor to be a part of the Violent Crimes Task Force with my fellow blue bloods and the FBI.

Would I risk my career and reputation because of Evelyn?

The old me met a hot artist at a coffee shop who conned me into believing her ghost stories. But the future me has the choice to go back to the way it was before that day.

Duke dropped his slobbery tennis ball at my feet. The big goofy dog grinned with his tongue hanging out of his mouth, waiting for me to throw the ball for the billionth time.

No matter how many times I threw the ball, Duke trotted after it and brought it back. I hoped he never found out he was retired. He loved to work, and even though chasing a ball was not as exciting as finding a missing person, Duke had a way of making his own fun.

I walked around the house as I pondered my life, with or

without Evelyn. She was an amazing person, but now that she was gone, the stress of having to answer to her and update her on my progress and do things to please her instead of myself lifted from my body.

Now that I was alone, I could breathe again. I headed upstairs to check out the bedrooms. There were three in total. It was a lot of space for two people, and I wondered if Evelyn and I had ever talked about having kids.

I loved my nieces and nephews, but I didn't see myself becoming a father. My career was too demanding and dangerous for a family man. As I thought about how I pictured my future, I made up my mind about my relationship with Evelyn.

My gut instinct was right—I would be better off without Evelyn in my life.

Breaking it off with her would be devastating to her and my family, but I had to do what was right for me—damn the consequences.

When I headed back downstairs, I suddenly felt dizzy. I stumbled on the stairs but grabbed the handrail and caught myself before I hit the ground.

As I took a few deep breaths to shake off the dizziness, an image of Professor Bradford flashed through my mind.

I was at the park again, but this time, the memory lasted longer. Nolan was holding a large brown paper bag. He tapped it on his knee nervously, reluctant to give it to me.

But just as he was about to hand it over, a searing pain pulsed through my head, tearing me out of the memory.

It took a few breaths to process what I thought had just happened. It was a memory from my attack. I was sure of it.

UNSTOPPABLE—EVELYN

I entered Bridgeport into my nav and hit the road.

It was a beautiful fall day and the warm and breezy weather was perfect for a road trip. I cranked up an upbeat country music playlist, rolled down the windows, and let the breeze blow through my hair.

I could feel my muscles relaxing. I did need to get away. I regretted that I had to miss my art show that evening, but there was no way I could stand in front of an audience and pretend everything was fine. My gallery manager, Gibson, was more than capable of running the show.

I sang along with the music as Kenny Chesney wooed me away from my problems. Since my near-death experience, life had taken me on a wild ride. But when I moved to Chicago and met Leo, I finally had someone who loved me enough to respect my mission in life and ride the ghost train with me.

We'll find our way back to each other, Leo. Don't give up on us.

I prepared for the trip with a tumbler of cold water, some

gas station snacks, and a box of tissues readily available on the passenger seat.

Traffic wasn't bad once I got out of town and headed toward the wide-open spaces of Indiana. While I had this time to myself, I did some soul-searching and imagined what my life would be like if my relationship with Leo ended.

Every morning when Leo opened his eyes, I hoped that his memory would return and our lives would go back to normal. I wanted him to see me as his fun-loving, loyal girlfriend instead of a burden he had to contend with.

Every day that passed, I worried the chances of Leo remembering the past were slim. I prayed that giving Leo space would help him focus on his health so he could return to work.

Before the attack, I was the most important person in his life, but now he had reverted to his old way of thinking. All he wanted was to return to work and get back to his old habits.

As I headed down the highway, my thoughts drifted to Dr. Vaughn. His phone call had come out of the blue, but the timing for a visit was oddly perfect.

I never thought I would hear from him again. But now that he had something important to talk to me about, I was curious to find out what had been going on in his life since he left the Windy City.

If Leo and I had not gotten into an argument and agreed to spend time apart, I would've never agreed to meet Dr. Vaughn at his house out in the sticks by myself. Leo and I would've gone together.

With the wind blowing through my hair and the blue skies ahead, I imagined what my future would look like if our relationship was beyond repair. I had my art, my career, and without Leo, no attachments to Chicago.

But that future never came fully into focus. Leo was my

life. There was no scenario where I would be better off, or happier, or more fulfilled, or free if he and I broke up.

I will never stop fighting for us, Leo.

No matter how rocky and busted up the road ahead of us was, I would fight for our love and do everything in my power to show him that his life would be better because we were together—not in spite of it.

Our love and commitment to one another was unstoppable. I already knew that. My job was to lead Leo back to me and prove to him that we were meant to be together—forever.

Losing Leo was the harshest reality I had ever faced in my life. In order to save our relationship, I had to prove to him that my gift was real all over again while giving him the time apart that he asked for. What I did know was that I believed I would find the evidence I needed to bring us back together when I deciphered the clue—Aurora.

WIDE OPEN—LEO

I closed my eyes and inhaled the steam from a hot shower. As I lathered up my body and soothed my aching muscles, I thought about Evelyn.

I remembered seeing her art show schedule on the door of the gallery and knew she had a show tonight. I didn't know if she had already left town to visit her friend, or if she would leave after her event.

Even though I planned to end our relationship, I didn't like not knowing where she was. It wasn't like I didn't care about her—I did—but since we had decided to separate for a couple of days, I wanted to honor our deal.

Evelyn can take care of herself.

Still, not knowing my girlfriend's whereabouts—and who she was with—went against my nature. I was a detective. I didn't like loose ends, but Evelyn had avoided my questions. She tried to sneak out of town without telling me where she was going, and when I asked her for details, she never revealed the identity of her mysterious friend.

I ran shampoo through my hair, careful not to press too hard on the knot on the back of my head, and massaged my temples to ease the pressure behind my ears. The only good thing that happened today was I got a snippet of a memory back.

Why had I agreed to meet Nolan Bradford, the main suspect in my missing person case, alone at the park without waiting for backup?

The answer was clear: I didn't go to meet Nolan. I went to the park to meet his wife, Cora. Evelyn and Parker both confirmed that's who I said I was meeting with, and I must've agreed because I never considered her a threat.

It pissed me off to think I was so stupid, but I reasoned that Nolan had somehow tricked me and lured me to the park under false pretenses, probably promising me information about the case.

But why would Nolan do that? To get even with me by conking me on the back of the head? That was the part that didn't add up. The guy had a vendetta against me, but he was an intelligent man who also knew I carried a gun.

Why would he come after me now, a year later, after Sloane's case had gone cold?

I took some deep breaths to get my blood flowing. I was missing some memories, but I was still a detective. My brain was trained to figure things out. Now that I remembered seeing Nolan at the park, the connection between my attack and the Sloane Matthews case was undeniably connected.

When I got out of the shower and toweled off, I thought about the crime scene photos and Evelyn's drawings. I still had no reasonable explanation for how Evelyn had gotten access to the evidence—or why she had sketched a picture of Sloane as a ghost.

However, Evelyn's drawing gave me a fresh perspective on the case.

The bonfire. We never checked the ashes for evidence or human remains. Evelyn's drawings showed personal items in the fire that we had collected from the woods. But in her sketch, she also revealed a melted face and bones being ravaged by fire.

What if Sloane's remains had been there under our noses the entire time? Was it possible my girlfriend had come up with a theory that would blow this case wide open?

I hated to admit it, but Evelyn was on to something.

BLAME—LEO

That evening, I called up Parker and Santoni to meet for dinner.

My partner was waiting at a corner booth with a round of PBRs on the table when I got there. I was hungry and eager to go over the new developments, so I picked one of my favorite neighborhood joints.

The place was hopping with regulars enjoying loaded Chicago-style pizza, hoagies, and baskets of chicken wings and deep-fried comfort food. Being in a familiar place eased my stress, and I was ready to celebrate the fact that small pieces of my memory had started to come back.

"Cheers!" Parker clinked my beer bottle. "I'm glad you're on the mend. The Team is ready for you to come back to work. It's not the same without you."

I took a swig of beer, then jumped right into the fresh details I remembered about the attack. "Nolan Bradford was there, and he was about to give me a large brown grocery bag. I lost the memory just before I saw what was inside."

My partner jotted down notes and then asked, "What

does Evelyn think about this? I'm sure she's thrilled your memories are coming back."

Here we go. The last person I wanted to talk about tonight was Evelyn. I needed a mental break from my relationship problems so I could focus on the case—especially now that I was remembering some details.

"Evelyn doesn't know yet."

"You didn't tell her?" Parker asked.

"She wasn't around when it happened. She's got some art thing at her gallery tonight."

Parker seemed genuinely confused. "She has an event at the gallery, and you didn't go?"

"I called you to go over new information about the case. I don't want to talk about my personal life."

"Fair enough." Parker lifted his hands apologetically.

I was ready to move on to my theory about the bonfire and the possibility that Sloane's remains might've been destroyed in the fire, but Parker's worried expression signaled his mind was still on Evelyn.

"What's with the face?" I snapped.

"I'm sorry. It's just—it's strange that you're not with Evelyn during one of her events. You've always been very protective—and supportive—of her in the past."

I sighed in frustration, knowing my partner would not let this go. "Evelyn and I had a disagreement yesterday. We're taking some time off."

Parker's eyes widened at the shock of my admission. "I know you don't want to talk about your personal life, but over the last year, we've become good friends. I'm concerned about you—and Evelyn. Talk to me, Leo."

I took a long swig of beer as I considered his request. "We got into a fight because I found out she lied to me about something important. When she stuck to her story, I said some things out of anger and told her we needed to take a break."

Parker plastered on his problem-solving face as he processed the facts. "What did Evelyn lie about?"

"Something strange. You know how she paints ghosts and draws all that creepy stuff?"

Parker nodded.

"Well, she tried to convince me that her ghosts are real. That these restless spirits visit her in her dreams and show her things. Then she draws pictures to help me solve their murders. She even sketched pictures of Sloane Matthews—as a corpse."

Parker's complexion paled. "How did you react when Evelyn told you this?"

"Exactly how you would imagine. I gave her a chance to come clean, but she stuck to her story. I don't believe in ghosts, so that was that. We need some time apart."

Parker looked horrified. "Where is Evelyn now?"

"I don't know. She might be at the gallery, or she might've already left to go out of town to visit a friend."

"What friend?" Parker asked.

"She didn't say."

"How bad was this fight?" Parker was a criminal profiler and had come face to face with cold-blooded psychopaths who showed no remorse for their crimes. He'd always kept his cool, but right now, he was clearly distressed about my fight with Evelyn.

An internal alarm went off inside my body, as dread and regret pulsed through my veins. Some things can never be unsaid, and the pain of knowing I'd hurt Evelyn needled away at my conscience.

"I was angry she lied to me. I said some things I can't take back."

"What did you say?"

When I gave him a recap of our argument and how Evelyn had interpreted my sentiment, Parker let out a sigh and leaned back in his seat as if a mule had kicked him in the chest.

"Hey, guys. What did I miss?" My buddy Santoni showed up and pulled up a chair.

"Leo and Evelyn had a fight—a bad one. He doesn't know where she is right now."

"What the fuck?" Santoni said.

"We had a disagreement," I said. "Couples fight, you know."

"Evelyn lied to him about her ghost drawings," Parker explained.

Santoni stared at me in disbelief. Not only had I disappointed myself and broken Evelyn's heart, I had lost the respect of the two guys in the world I considered my best friends.

Parker gave Santoni the quick and dirty version of the situation to catch him up to speed.

"We need to find her," Santoni said.

Even though I knew the guys had my best interests at heart, I didn't want them involved in my personal life. I was responsible for my own actions—my relationship with Evelyn wasn't a group project.

"I appreciate your help, but I need to do this on my own." I opened the app on my phone and tracked her location. "Evelyn's at her art gallery. I'll talk to her before she leaves to visit her friend out of town." I pointed to her location on Halsted.

Santoni took control of the situation before I fucked up any further.

"Listen, buddy. Evelyn's telling the truth about her gift. Parker and I are the only other people in the world who know about her automatic drawings. We believe her, and you believe her—you just don't remember."

"We don't expect you to understand everything right now," Parker said. "But it will all make sense in time. Evelyn is not a liar. She never meant to hurt you. The reason she was being evasive about her gift was because she feared you would push her away."

"IF ANYONE IS to blame for this, you can point your finger at the two of us," Santoni said. "We discussed this with Evelyn, and the three of us agreed not to tell you about the true nature of her gift."

"You experienced a brain injury," Parker added. "We thought it was best not to drop this on you while you were recovering. We all expected your memory would come back before it became an issue."

"I'm sorry, Leo," Santoni said. "We made the wrong choice."

I was confused as hell, but I believed my friends wouldn't steer me wrong. While I still didn't have all the answers, one thing was clear. I needed to find Evelyn.

I rushed to the gallery where Evelyn's art show was in full swing.

I didn't remember going to any of her shows in the past and was surprised to see Evelyn's fun and artsy personality reflected in her party.

There was a cocktail server wearing a devil costume, delivering elevated Bloody Mary cocktails to the high-end clientele. Each drink was garnished with a mini slider with Evelyn's initials branded on the bun.

As I cruised through the crowd in search of Evelyn, a trio of musicians played a jazzy, syncopated version of Highway to Hell. I got a lot of looks from Evelyn's inner art circle, possibly because they knew me, but I didn't have the time or patience for small talk.

I maneuvered through the crowd and checked every partitioned section of the gallery. Along the way, I marveled at Evelyn's paintings and admired her artistic talent.

The paintings were all unique but had a common theme: The Devil in Disguise, Evelyn's fall collection. Based on the show announcement I'd seen in the window, tonight was a preview party for her gallery patrons and clients ahead of her Final Friday Gallery Walk coming up next week.

When I had cleared every room, a tall woman with platinum blond hair rushed up to greet me.

"Leo! So glad you're here. You look well." The woman, Gibson, according to her name badge, had a million-dollar smile and seemed genuinely glad to see me.

Evelyn had mentioned her name, and I remembered Gibson was the gallery manager who was blowing up her phone about the details of tonight's event. "I'm looking for Evelyn. Have you seen her?"

Gibson's smile faded. "No. She said she had to go out of town unexpectedly and couldn't make it tonight. I assumed she was leaving with you."

"Right. That's my mistake. I will relay to Evelyn how you packed the house tonight. Have a good evening."

I was about to leave, but something was off. I pulled out my phone and checked the app to locate Evelyn's phone. Once again, her cell pinged at the gallery and pinpointed her location.

The same location her phone had been since yesterday afternoon.

I waited until a guest distracted Gibson, then slipped upstairs to check Evelyn's studio. When I reached the door, it was locked. I knocked.

No answer.

A million horrible thoughts crossed my mind as I pulled out my pocketknife and jimmied the lock. I had unjustly accused her of being a liar and fraud. What if she had taken an emotional turn for the worse?

Apparently, the old me made sure Evelyn's studio was a safe and secure space for her. After what Evelyn had gone through, I wouldn't have expected anything less than high security. But now that I was trying to break in, I was kicking myself for not installing a retinal scanner that would have given me easy access.

Almost there…snap!

Once I was inside, I turned on the lights and searched the room. Evelyn wasn't there. I called her phone and listened. I followed the vibration to her desk and opened the drawer.

Evelyn had left her phone behind.

She must've known I would keep tabs on her and left her cell to make me think she was still here. I had to give her props for duping the detective, but as I considered the reason, my heart filled with guilt as her motive became clear.

Evelyn didn't want me to find her.

The bigger question was, why?

Evelyn had a four-digit security code on her phone. If she ever gave it to me, it was lost somewhere in my memories. But I was observant by nature. I made a living out of noticing things other people may have overlooked.

When I entered a room, I counted the number of people, located the exit and entry points, observed signs of suspicious behavior, and identified potential threats in about five seconds flat.

That being said, I memorized Evelyn's password the first time I saw her tap it in after she took me home from the hospital. It wasn't for any other reason than I wanted to know, in case I ever needed to use it—like now.

1-0-3-1. Halloween day. A spooky code for the ghost girl who made a living off painting the dead.

I took people's rights seriously, but my gut told me Evelyn needed me. If she never wanted to speak to me again because I accessed her phone without permission, fine, but if Evelyn needed help, it was a risk I was willing to take.

I searched her call log and recent messages.

When I checked the history, it shocked me to see a name I recognized from the past. Not that I remembered him personally, but his name was all over one of my old cases—Dr. Vaughn Reynolds.

EVELYN: On my way! See you in three hours.

Why the fuck is Evelyn going on a road trip to visit him?

SCRAPS—EVELYN

r. Vaughn waved from the front porch of his rustic log cabin.

He was dressed in a flannel shirt, faded jeans, and hiking boots—the total opposite style of his once dapper, polished appearance one would expect from Chicago's most successful heart surgeon.

Vaughn's formerly neat and perfectly coiffed blonde hair had grown long, and his meticulously groomed beard was now bushy and wild, like his new homestead. His appearance and style were different, but his genuine smile and intelligent eyes lit up as I rolled into the driveway.

Seeing my friend thriving in his new world warmed my heart. After all Vaughn had gone through, I was thrilled to see him coming out of his horror story with a new take on life. My upbeat and positive attitude had gone dormant, and I was grateful Vaughn had reached out and invited me to visit.

"Dr. Vaughn!" I hopped out of the car and rushed to give him a hug. When I wrapped my arms around him, I noted he was rocking a new muscular physique to match his mountain-man persona. His beefed-up body was strong and well-defined, and I couldn't wait to hear what he'd been doing with his life since his departure from Chicago.

When Vaughn released me from his bear hug, he pulled back and studied my expression. I couldn't mask my puffy face and red nose or erase the worry lines and dark circles from under my eyes.

Vaughn was a gentleman. Instead of grilling me about my health or asking me questions I wasn't ready to answer, he simply said, "I'm glad you're here, Evelyn."

I gave him an appreciative smile as he grabbed my bag and led me inside.

After I got settled in, Vaughn led me to his back porch. He poured a couple of glasses of his home-brewed beer and set out some savory snacks. The weather was gorgeous, and a warmer than usual fall breeze blew through the trees and scattered colorful leaves in the backyard.

A murder of crows kept tabs on us from the treetops, cawing to each other in bird speak, gossiping about the new girl. I imagined them squawking about my shiny crystal pendants and complimenting the ghoulish Jack-o'-lantern design on my spooky scarf.

"I think my birds like you, Evelyn."

"Your birds?"

"They're the only friends I have out here." Vaughn teased. He seemed in good spirits, and I hoped he was healing from the tragedy of losing his wife. His home in the woods was peaceful and serene, but his new life seemed more like an escape than a fresh start.

"What have you been doing since you left the city?" I was eager to learn why he wanted to see me so desperately but didn't want to immediately come out and ask him why he wanted me here so badly.

Vaughn stared into the clear blue sky as he considered his

response. "That's just it, Evelyn. I've been experiencing something unusual."

"What's happening?"

"Come inside. I need to show you something."

His décor was sparse, but he had a nice collection of beer glasses and steins along a wooden shelf in the kitchen.

Vaughn led me to his kitchen table. He folded his hands, collected his thoughts, and then looked me in the eye. "I hear words in my head, Evelyn. Specifically, the same word on an endless loop. At first, I believed I was suffering from a sort of psychosis, but as the word came more frequently—"

Vaughn gathered his thoughts. "I realized it wasn't random. The word was a message."

Holy crap.

I rubbed my arms to chase away the goosebumps. I knew all too well what Vaughn was experiencing—a clairaudient message—but I didn't want to influence his opinion by sharing my expertise on the matter. "What word did you hear?"

Vaughn retrieved an envelope and emptied the contents onto the table. There were random pieces of paper and pages torn from magazines and books, with Vaughn's handwriting scrolled across every inch of the papers.

As I examined the pile, I was shocked to see Vaughn had written the same word on every single paper, over and over and over. I broke into a cold sweat as I stared at what I believed was a paranormal phenomenon.

"I heard the word in my head, but I have no memory of writing it down, Evelyn. It happened one night after I went to bed. I live alone. No one broke into my house. This was done by my hand, but I don't know why or what it means."

"Did anything else happen leading up to this?"

Vaughn's eyes glistened with a combination of fright and

enthusiasm. "During the night, I had a dream. It was so vivid, I would swear it actually happened in real life."

"What did you dream about?"

Vaughn's expression turned serious. "I dreamed of you, Evelyn, but you were different. Your hair. Your clothes. The way you carried yourself was off from the way you are now. But make no mistake. It was you in my dream and—"

"What? Tell me. In the dream, was I alone, or was someone with me? Give me every detail you remember."

Vaughn considered my question. "Leo wasn't with you, but I saw a blur of people in the background. I couldn't make out any faces aside from yours."

Vaughn leaned back in his chair and ran his fingers through his hair. "I can't explain why, but I know this message is meant for you." He tapped his finger over the scattered papers. "Tell me I'm not crazy, Evelyn. Does this word mean anything to you?"

I stared at the pile of papers. Vaughn must've written the word over a thousand times on various scraps of paper.

Aurora.

SLAMMED—LEO

The apartment was empty without Evelyn.

I paced the living room and stared at her army of scented candles as I contemplated my next move.

I played back the last time I saw her. Evelyn had put on a brave face, but I could tell she was an emotional wreck. My harsh words and accusations cut her to the bone, and I was certain seeing me with Rochelle conjured up scathing images in her head.

How could I have been so insensitive?

That alone was enough of a reason to track her down. She deserved a real apology, and I didn't like the idea that she went out of town to meet another man. Not only that, Parker and Santoni were convinced her gift was the real deal.

If that was true, I had a lot of questions. I trusted my partner and best friend with my life, but the idea that she could communicate with the dead was hard to swallow. I still had my doubts, but Evelyn honestly believed she could communicate with the dead through her art.

From her point of view, she was telling me the truth.

Fuck. What am I supposed to do now?

The dog was laying in the foyer, pointing his nose at the door, waiting for Evelyn to come home. Shit. Even the dog was making me feel guilty.

I hadn't changed my mind about my future with Evelyn. Since the assault, every aspect of my life revolved around the spooky artist with bright blue eyes, gorgeous long hair, and a rocking body that got my blood pumping whenever she came near me.

I understood my attraction to Evelyn. What I couldn't wrap my head around was why I'd dove headfirst into Evelyn's macabre lifestyle and compromised my morals by feeding into her ghost stories.

"Come here, Duke." The big boy trotted over and sat beside me obediently. His big eyes shined as I petted him and told him he was a good boy.

"Do you miss Evelyn?" When I said her name, Duke lifted his ears and cocked his head.

Christ. He knows her name.

I lifted Evelyn's sketchbook off the coffee table and mindlessly flipped through the pages. The trust we once shared had been destroyed, so I felt no remorse as I snooped through her private sketches.

Duke recognized Evelyn's scent and sniffed the book.

The dog had a long career as a search and rescue K9. Now that I had a home with a fenced-in backyard, I hoped Duke's handler and her new husband would bring him over for a visit once I got settled into the new place.

My thoughts drifted back to Evelyn. After talking to my friends, I hadn't changed my mind about our relationship. She was a wonderful and interesting person, but I never wanted to be tied down.

The sooner I could end things, the better off both of us would be. I could get back on the job and finish remodeling the house. Evelyn could focus on her amazing career as she healed emotionally from our breakup.

Someone knocked on the door.

Duke sat at attention and cocked his head.

I went to answer it, hoping it was Evelyn, but when I squinted through the peephole, I found another woman who deserved my apology—Mom.

I opened the door and was greeted with a warm and loving hug. "You sure know how to make me worry. How are you? Did you get enough to eat today?"

No matter that I was a detective and had lived on my own for over ten years, I would always be Mom's baby. "Yeah, all good. Sorry I didn't come over today." I kissed her on the cheek and invited her inside.

Mom's expression was loaded with concern. "How's my baby?"

"Your baby is a grown man. I'm fine."

"Headaches?"

"The mom job doesn't end, does it?"

"No. Answer me, Leo."

I sighed. "Sometimes. What do you expect me to say? I'm going about my life. No coddling, please."

"Good. Because you need to hear something." Mom grabbed my hands and pressed them against her heart. "You know how much I love you, son?"

"Why are you saying that? Of course, I do."

"When I found out you got hurt, I rushed to the hospital. All the doctors said I couldn't see you. I didn't know what was going on, and I was so worried I didn't know what to do."

"I know that was rough. I'm sorry you had to go through that."

"But when Evelyn got there, she took control of that entire emergency room. She tracked down the E.R. doctor for an update, then insisted they bring in a head trauma specialist from another hospital to take over your case."

Damn. No one told me that.

"And once she and your fellow bluebloods had everyone in the hospital on notice that a brave Chicago P.D. hero needed the best care in the city, Evelyn comforted me. She promised me you were going to be alright because she was going to take care of you."

"That's nice, Mom."

"I closed my eyes and thanked God for sending us Evelyn. My heart was full of gratitude, knowing you were safe in her hands. I was so relieved that you finally found your soulmate. When the staff gave me this, I knew you felt the same way."

Mom reached into her purse and placed a small velvet box in my hand. I popped the top and found an engagement ring inside.

"You had that in your coat pocket when they brought you to the hospital," Mom said. "You were going to propose to Evelyn that night."

I stared at the ring as if the sparkling diamond solitaire held the secrets of the universe. Every time I tried to move a step further away from Evelyn, an unstoppable force slammed us back together.

"Leo, I know you value your privacy. Everyone knows you value your privacy." She smirked. "I'm going to leave now so that you can process this in your own Leo way. Just know that I love you and want what's best for you, always."

I walked her to her car, but we stayed silent, and she left quickly. I was grateful for that. I went back inside and sat with my thoughts. And the ring. A fucking engagement ring, from Leo Ricci. Who would've ever predicted that?

But who could've predicted someone like Evelyn Sinclair?

My head was telling me to move on from my relationship

with Evelyn. If I followed the lead of my busted-up brain, my life would be a hell of a lot less complicated.

The trouble was that my heart was leading me in a different direction. Without Evelyn, a part of me was missing. No matter how many excuses I made or how hard I tried to convince myself, my soul ached for the cool and edgy artist I couldn't get out of my head.

Evelyn and I were destined to be together. The sooner I faced that reality, the sooner we could move past the heartache and get back to where we belonged—together.

I patted the dog on the back. "Come on, Duke. Let's bring Evelyn home."

PREMONITION—EVELYN

$\mathcal{D}$r. Vaughn and I stayed up late discussing the paranormal epiphany.

I confided with him about my relationship problems with Leo, and Dr. Vaughn was a kind and compassionate listener. As a doctor, he believed Leo was suffering from a loss of control stemming from his amnesia, and it was normal for him to lash out at the people he loved during his health crisis.

I trusted Vaughn, and my heart ached knowing Leo was suffering. I had sworn to his mother I would take care of him while he heeled, and I did the worst possible thing—I left him.

Part of me felt selfish for running away, but Leo couldn't stand to be in the same room with me. I hoped a few days apart would give us both time to regroup and come together to find a positive solution to our problems.

I spent the night in Vaughn's guest room and tossed and turned all night as I replayed everything Vaughn and I had discussed. In the early morning, when the roosters declared it was the dawn of a new day, I thought of something the doctor and I had not yet considered.

Vaughn's vision of me wasn't a dream—it was a premonition.

He saw my future without Leo in it—I was alone because Leo was gone. I hopped out of bed and paced the room, desperate to come up with a different conclusion, but nothing else made sense.

No way.

I would never let him go. My mission from that moment forward was to stop this premonition from coming to pass. The universe was going to a lot of trouble to deliver this message, but this time I would have to unravel the clues and solve the mystery without Leo's help.

Think, Evelyn...As I considered how the crime was connected to my relationship with Leo, the answer became alarmingly clear—Leo's life was in danger.

What if Leo and I weren't together because he was no longer alive?

Nolan Bradford was still on the loose. Since he had a vendetta against Leo, he might be hiding out, waiting to strike again.

Not on my watch.

Leo expected me to be gone for a few days. While we were apart, I would track the clues and find out the meaning of the message. Solving the crime and outing Leo's attacker could end up saving his life—and possibly bring us back together.

While I had planned to spend a few days with Vaughn, I couldn't kick back and relax now that I knew Leo needed my help. Once daylight broke, Vaughn left the cabin to go for a run. I decided it was best to leave before he returned. If I explained why I was leaving, Vaughn would undoubtedly try to talk me out of it.

So, I left a note on the kitchen counter before I left, thanking him for all he'd done for me. Vaughn was a good friend, and I was grateful he had the courage to deliver the message I was destined to hear.

As I made my getaway, a committee of vultures circled above. Their shadows cast over the road ahead as I headed back to the highway.

I'll do whatever it takes to save Leo.

HOSTILE—LEO

Contacting Dr. Vaughn wasn't a winning game plan.

My career in law enforcement taught me that there were only three ways a person reacted when they knew they were busted.

The first reaction was the most obvious—they lied. I couldn't count the number of perps and felons I had convicted over the years, and nine times out of ten, when I asked a guilty person a question, even an easy one, they lied to my face.

I'm not saying Dr. Vaughn was a criminal or that he had done anything wrong. But until I found out why my girlfriend went on a road trip to meet up with a smart and successful friend from her past after we had gotten into a big fight, I would treat the good doctor as a hostile witness.

The second most common reaction—they would run.

If I called Vaughn, and he tipped off Evelyn that I was looking for her, she might take off. In the short time that I'd gotten to know her, I learned she hated conflict.

Evelyn bolted the moment she felt unloved, and I didn't want to risk chasing her off before I could talk to her in person. I needed to use the element of surprise and catch her off guard.

The third reaction was less common—the guilty person would confess. If I called Dr. Vaughn and asked him why my girlfriend had run to him after our fight, he might tell me something I didn't want to hear.

I had no evidence to support my suspicions, but my detective's brain kept asking the same question: "Why did Evelyn leave me to meet another man?"

A handsome, charming, wealthy heart surgeon who called Evelyn out of the blue the moment the news hit that I had been injured in the line of duty. I didn't believe Evelyn would cheat on me.

However, I wasn't confident that a lonely guy who lived way the fuck out in the middle of the woods wouldn't make a move on my girlfriend while she was feeling crappy about herself.

Duke and I hit the road early the next morning. Dr. Vaughn's place was three hours away from Chicago. If we only took a short break, we would reach his place while Evelyn was still sipping her cappuccino.

I rolled down the windows and turned on some classic rock music. As I sang along with Springsteen, we crossed the border into Indiana. The road was flat, and there was nothing but farmland and windmills for miles. With my eyes on the road ahead, a calming sense of serenity lifted my spirits.

I'm on the right path.

As I cruised down the highway, Duke sniffed the air and panted happily as we headed toward Bridgemont, Indiana. My stomach was growling, so I veered off the exit to grab a quick breakfast.

I went through the Starbucks drive-thru and ordered a black coffee and an egg sandwich. The cashier gave me a puzzled look when she handed me my order. "Is that all you want?"

"What else do I need?"

"You didn't order a Puppuccino." She shot a pitiful look at the dog.

"What's a Puppuccino?" I glanced over at Duke. He had a long string of drool dangling from his lips.

Five seconds later, I was holding a green and white cup filled with whipped cream. K9 Duke wagged his tail as he licked the cup clean and enjoyed his special treat. The dog still wore his old K9 harness like a badge of honor. The cashier waved goodbye and thanked the dog for his service as we pulled away.

Parker was keeping me updated on the search for Nolan Bradford. My memory was sketchy, and I still couldn't ID the person who attacked me. The professor had been there, but the details surrounding what happened were a blur.

Still, Chicago P.D. and the FBI were using all their resources to find him, and his wife, Cora, to bring them in for questioning. Since I was off duty and the victim in the case, I wasn't officially involved in the investigation.

My partner kept reminding me to watch my back. The person who attacked me was still on the loose. Someone had whacked me over the head for a reason, and until we found out why, Parker believed I was still in danger.

While I thought about the details of the case, my partner called. "Hey, Parker."

"Were you able to locate Evelyn?" he asked.

"I know where she is, but I haven't spoken to her. Why?"

"There's been a development in your case. I went to the gallery to talk to Evelyn's manager about Nolan. Considering he has a vendetta against you, I wanted to cover all my bases and check to see if she had ever seen him, lurking around the gallery."

"What did she say?"

"I showed Gibson a picture of him. The professor didn't look familiar, but she recognized his name. Nolan Bradford signed the guest book last night at Evelyn's art show."

"Are you fucking kidding me? I was there last night." Anger boiled my blood at the idea that Nolan had been following me, and I led him straight to Evelyn.

"There's more. Someone placed a photo on the table beside the book. It was a picture of Evelyn walking the dog. I can't confirm these two pieces of evidence are connected, but we need to get eyes on Evelyn as soon as possible."

"I agree, but I'm having a hard time seeing Nolan Bradford strolling into Evelyn's art show, signing his name in the guest book, and yanking my chain by placing a photo of my girlfriend at the scene. Are there any other suspects in my case?"

Parker agreed. It seemed like a setup. "No one has been able to ID Nolan Bradford either at the park during the assault or at the art gallery. I've had my doubts since the investigation began, but now that you remember seeing him at the park, we need to find out why he was there."

"Any leads on his whereabouts? What about his wife, Cora?" I pressed the gas pedal and veered into the left lane to get past a line of Sunday drivers.

"No. We're doing everything we can to find them both. Can you come up with anyone else who might have a vendetta against you?"

"I'll think it over. I'm on my way to Evelyn's location now. I'll be there in thirty minutes."

"Good. Let me know when you reach her."

"One more thing. The cadaver dogs got a hit at the bonfire. I have a forensic team there now collecting evidence. There were no bones visible in the debris, but three different

K9s all signaled human remains in the ashes. There may be DNA we can use to confirm the victim."

"Good work, Partner. Keep me updated."

Holy shit. The only reason I mentioned the bonfire to Parker was because of Evelyn's drawing. Her claims about communicating with the dead were spookier than fiction, but her art produced a lead and possibly steered us toward the body of a missing person.

THE THOUGHT OF SLOANE MATTHEWS' ghost communicating with Evelyn through her art gave me chills, but the evidence was adding up. I could no longer dismiss Evelyn's gift as a figment of her imagination.

HORROR STORY—EVELYN

The most obvious starting point was Aurora, Indiana, so I hit the highway and headed south.

Still, I couldn't shake off my instincts telling me I was searching for a thing or a person, not a place. I thought about my drawings and how they connected.

The sketch of Sloane wearing a costume made sense because she disappeared on Halloween night while attending a bonfire party. Those two sketches validated the identity of my ghost and the location where she was last seen.

But what about the antique doll collection? How was I supposed to pull a clue from a pile of old dolls?

When I reached a small town called Grandview, I pulled off the exit to get something to eat. I was starving, and something about the town's sign pulled me to it. "Grandview, where kindness is our way of life."

Next to the sign, there was a scarecrow family sitting on hay bales, a huge display of pumpkins and gourds, along with a fun variety of family-friendly yard stakes featuring cartoonish witches and glittery black cats.

I parked in the historic district of the small town and

took a walk to stretch my legs in the quaint Midwestern town. There was an ice cream shop on the corner, an antique store, a bakery, and a restaurant with a wooden menu board on the sidewalk in front of the entrance.

I studied the sign and mentally applauded the artist's chalkboard design. The hand-drawn font was colorful bubble letters that read Daily Specials. It listed the features with bullet point hearts followed by a thick white script to make the menu pop.

Prime rib with mashed potatoes, fried chicken dinner with all the fixings, mac and cheese with fall vegetables, and a portabella burger with sweet potato fries. For dessert: Caroline's pumpkin cheesecake.

Sold.

When I entered the restaurant, a pink-haired hostess greeted me and asked how many people were in my party.

"One." I held up a finger. "I'm having lunch by myself today."

The stylish teen grabbed a menu and led me to a small wooden table by the window with a perfect view of the street. A storm was rolling in, and the sky was a gloomy shade of gray.

The setting matched my mood. I hadn't eaten a decent meal or slept since our fight. I was physically and emotionally drained, and my body felt dull and heavy from exhaustion.

I studied the drink menu and contemplated whether or not to order a cocktail. An alcoholic beverage sounded amazing, but I needed to stay mentally sharp and opted for a caffeinated beverage.

When the server arrived, I ordered mac and cheese, a fresh fruit cup, and a Coke.

"Is that it?" The woman with short gray hair tapped her pan on her waitress pad.

"I'm saving room for dessert," I replied.

"We have the best pumpkin cheesecake in town. The recipe has been in my family for generations."

"You must be Caroline." My gaze slid to her name badge to confirm.

"I'll set a slice aside for you and bring it out when you finish your meal."

I thanked her, then leaned back in my chair and exhaled a deep breath. I studied the restaurant's décor, from the line of ceramic roosters lined up on the shelves above the windows to the ruffly sheer curtains with a barnyard design on the fabric.

The bell on the door jangled, and a group of friends entered the restaurant, waved to Caroline, and then planted themselves at the bar and ordered a round of afternoon cocktails.

While I was watching the group get settled in, I noticed the twenty-something-year-old bartender sneaking glances at me. I gave him a polite smile and turned my attention out the window.

I noticed my reflection in the glass. Black jacket zipped up to my chin, baseball cap, sunglasses—I looked like a female version of the Unabomber. Nonchalantly, I slid off my sunglasses, so he didn't think I was a fugitive.

A few moments later, I peeked over to see if the guy was still watching me. Thankfully, his customers were keeping him busy. The blender was whirling, and he was busy pouring drinks and making small talk with the customers.

Rain started pouring, and the townsfolk on the sidewalk darted under the awning to take cover. People were laughing and—

"Hey, how's it going?"

I turned around and found the bartender standing beside me with a frozen drink in hand.

"Hi. Good. Uh, I didn't order that."

"On the house. I made a little extra and thought you might like to try it." He pushed his hair back and gave me an adorable smile. He had a clean-shaven face and a deep dimple on the right side of his cheek.

Is he flirting with me?

Dating a detective has given me a wealth of knowledge about how victims of violent crimes were snared by predators. Leo's deep voice boomed in my head…

"Never accept a drink from a stranger. I could give you a list of all the drugs a sexual predator could lace your cocktail with to render you helpless…."

"No thanks. I don't drink." The bartender wasn't trying to drug me, for goodness' sake, but I stuck to my guns about needing to stay alert.

"No problem. I'm Dillon, by the way. If you decide you want something else, just wave me down."

When he went back to work, I pulled a pen out of my purse and decided to draw until my food arrived. I flipped over the paper placemat and doodled an abstract design, using the elemental energy of the storm to fuel my creative muse.

As my hand moved across the page, all my thoughts were on Leo. His apology was sincere, and he asked me not to go. Had I made a mistake by leaving?

No. I needed time to recover from our fight. Historically in our relationship, Leo called all the shots. Denying him when he asked me not to go was my way of showing him I could make my own decisions.

A loud burst of thunder rumbled the windows.

When I closed my eyes, all my thoughts drifted back to Leo. As I thought about him and how much I missed our home, my hand moved across the page.

· · ·

"Miss…Miss?" A hand touched my shoulder, causing me to jump out of my skin. I must've zoned out while I was drawing.

I opened my eyes and found Caroline delivering my order. "Oh. Sorry. I didn't see you there." I leaned back so she could set down my plate, but she drew back when she saw my spooky work of art.

I'd sketched a horrific picture of Sloane Matthews. Her mouth was open wide as if she had screamed her last breath. The ghost pressed her hands against her cheeks in a desperate attempt to keep her severed head attached to her body.

Sloane was here, in this restaurant, standing in front of the bar. A pool of blood oozed over the floor, and the background of my drawing looked like a photographic image of this setting—minus the horror story.

RECKLESS—LEO

I slid off my shades as I rolled into Dr. Vaughn's driveway.

There was a man on the front porch of the log cabin, wearing a flannel shirt and jeans. He had a knife in hand, peeling and slicing a bowl of apples.

I glanced down at the photo of Vaughn from my Windy City files and looked back at the guy on the porch. It was definitely Dr. Reynolds—but he looked nothing like the man I had once considered a suspect in his wife's murder investigation.

He grinned when I stepped out of my vehicle.

"Good morning, Vaughn." I didn't know how the guy would react to seeing me, but he didn't seem surprised I was there.

"Detective Ricci, you look well. Good to see you're recovering." Dr. Vaughn dried his hands on a dish towel and met me in the driveway. He offered a handshake and a smile, so I responded in kind.

"I'm here to see Evelyn."

"I'm afraid you missed her. She left earlier this morning."

Evelyn's car wasn't in the driveway, but that didn't mean she was gone. Maybe she expected a visit from me and tried to cover her tracks like she had with her phone.

"Where did she go? Back to Chicago?"

"She didn't say."

The good doctor was tightlipped, but I wasn't giving up on the only lead I had to Evelyn's location. She might've been headed home, but she very well might've been on her way to somewhere else entirely. "It's been a long trip. Do you mind if I let the dog run for a while before I leave?"

Dr. Vaughn smiled when he saw the dog riding shotgun. "Hey, buddy." He reached inside the car and greeted the big boy. "I've got plenty of room for him to run. Can I offer you a beer?"

It wasn't even noon yet, but a beer sounded great. We made small talk in the kitchen as I watched the dog from the window. Then I got to the point of my visit. "Why did Evelyn come here?"

Vaughn considered my question before answering. "I invited her."

"Why?"

"The timing seemed right."

"Do you mean the timing of my amnesia, or the timing of our argument?"

Dr. Vaughn let out a chuckle. "You haven't changed a bit, Detective. Regarding your head trauma, you may not be seeing things clearly right now. I mean this respectfully, Leo, but I want to explain something that you may not fully comprehend, considering your memory loss."

Vaughn tapped his fingers on the table. "Evelyn would do anything for you. She would put your best interests above her own without hesitation. She would never let any harm come to you. Do you understand what I'm saying?"

"In theory, yes. But what's your point?"

"When Evelyn arrived, she looked as if she'd hit rock bottom. There was no joy in her expression, and I knew the moment I saw her that something had happened in your relationship. There is only one person on this earth who could've taken the spark from her eyes. That person is you."

I was pissed Dr. Vaughn had the nerve to weigh in our relationship. "Look, we had an argument. I was wrong. I came here to find her so I could fix things between us. I don't know what she told you—"

"Nothing. She didn't speak an ill word about you, which brings me to my point. I'm worried about her. I have a feeling she's doing something reckless to help you or your relationship," the doctor said.

"Her greatest fear is losing you, and something tells me she is chasing something or someone who could bring the two of you back together. Does that make sense?"

For some strange reason, it did. "Be more specific? What is Evelyn chasing? Where is she going? Tell me everything you know. Even something small may turn into a lead."

Dr. Vaughn's gaze landed on a large envelope that was sitting at the breakfast table. "I called Evelyn because I had information about something important, but now I regret—"

"What information?"

Vaughn clenched his jaw as if trying to stop himself from telling me something he shouldn't.

"If Evelyn is in danger, I have to help her."

Vaughn moved to the table and picked up the envelope. "Does the word Aurora mean anything to you, Detective?"

MISTAKE—EVELYN

"*O*h, my. That's quite a drawing," Caroline said as she scrutinized my work.

I flipped over the sketch and made light of my dark artistic style. "I guess the stormy weather put me in the Halloween spirit."

Caroline set my food down and scurried off. I glanced around the room to see if anyone else had noticed what I had drawn, but everyone seemed to be in their own element.

The bartender was polishing glasses and hadn't seemed to notice.

Be more careful, Evelyn.

I picked up my fork and stabbed a macaroni noodle. I took a few bites, but I was too anxious to eat. I glanced back at the bartender and busted him watching me again.

His vibe made me nervous.

Suddenly, a number popped into my head—117.

Leave, Evelyn. Now.

I left some money on the table, grabbed my drawing, and bolted for the door. On my way to my car, raindrops pelted my face as I made my getaway. Something about the bartender or that place had raised the hair on the back of my neck.

I don't know what or who had me spooked, but I had an overwhelming urge to run and leave this place. But I couldn't. I'd had the sense to turn off in this town, and then my sketch was clearly linking Sloane to this very restaurant. I couldn't leave. I was close to something—I could feel it.

Once I made it to my car, I made a plan. Check into a hotel, get some rest, and figure out my next move. As I checked the rearview mirror before pulling into traffic, someone banged on my passenger-side car window, scaring a yelp out of me.

I tried to see who it was, but the windows were fogged up from the storm. It didn't matter who it was—I didn't know a soul in this town. I ran my hand along the door to hit the lock, but before I could, the passenger door opened.

"Hey, there. You forgot your dessert!" The bartender, Dillon, set the carryout box on my seat. "Have a good day." He shut the door and left just as quickly as he'd come.

I pressed my hand over my heart as I panted to catch my breath.

Be more careful, Evelyn. You're alone now. Don't make the same mistake again.

CROSSROADS—LEO

After Dr. Vaughn had dropped the paranormal bomb on me, I needed some time to process the information.

My aim was to find Evelyn. Her last known location was Vaughn's cabin in the woods. The last time he saw her was when they went to separate bedrooms for the night. She left a note telling him goodbye before she hit the road. She had no cell phone to track, didn't tell Vaughn where she was going, and had not contacted any of our friends or family.

The only clues I had to go on were Vaughn's bizarre automatic writings, and Evelyn's drawings from her sketchbook. The common thread that tied the two things together was a single word—Aurora.

The key to finding Evelyn was deciphering that clue.

When I left Vaughn's, I pulled over at a rest stop and studied Evelyn's sketches. If her drawings served as clues, I needed to find out what they meant so I could track her down.

There were four drawings in total:

Sloane Mathews in her costume—post-mortem.

The bonfire with melted body parts.

A collection of creepy antique dolls.

And one I had found in Evelyn's sketchbook of a wolf peeking around a tree.

I had already found numerical clues and the word Aurora in the first three drawings. At first glance, no words or numbers popped out in the wolf picture.

Look harder, Ricci. Follow the patterns…

I started at the top left corner and tracked my finger across the page as if reading a book. I repeated the process until I found the number "one" hidden on a tree trunk.

I repeated the process until I found another number on the wolf and one on the horizon line. When put in order, I got a three-digit number—117.

It went against my skeptical nature, but I needed help with this unbelievable paranormal matter. I called Parker and told him everything about my visit with Dr. Vaughn and how it related to Evelyn.

"Fascinating," Parker said. "Put the drawings in chronological order. Send me a picture of all of them together, then each one individually."

Parker was one of the sharpest minds on the task force. He was quick to make an assessment and said that this was something we did with Evelyn all the time. He even mentioned that her drawings had helped us solve multiple murder investigations.

Still, the idea of this blew my mind.

After a minute of me texting and Parker viewing the sketches on his phone, we were back at it. "What do the drawings have in common?" Parker asked. "I see a set of lines in each sketch. Rearrange the pictures and see if they line up."

This is fucking crazy.

I had the drawings spread out in the trunk of my car and

followed his line of reasoning. When I changed the order of the drawings and connected the lines, I stepped back and made a connection.

"Holy shit." I snapped a picture and sent it to Parker. "Am I nuts, or do you see a road map?" I stared at the lines that looked a hell of a lot like the highway. Evelyn had even drawn the faintest outline of crossroads and exit markers.

"Nice work, Detective. What else do you see?"

My heart pounded with excitement when I spotted four abstract stars randomly placed on the sketches. "See the stars?" I asked him. "The drawings are a road map. Each one corresponds with a highway exit. Do you think this is where Evelyn is headed?"

"I'd bet my reputation on it, Leo. How close are you to the first star?"

"A couple exits away. I'm getting back on the road now."

"Agreed. I'll contact all the hotels and B&Bs at each exit. Do you want me to meet you there?"

"No. the fourth star is back in Chicago. Stay there in case she comes back. If Evelyn contacts anyone, I want to know about it."

I pulled up the navigation, set my location, and peeled out of the rest stop like a bat out of hell.

Grandview, Indiana. Here I come.

INSTINCTS—EVELYN

When I checked into the hotel, I grabbed some brightly colored brochures from the visitor's station and hustled back to the safety of my room. I needed to calm my mind and figure out my next steps.

As I chomped down on a king-size candy bar to satisfy my hunger, my mind drifted back to the restaurant—and my horrid drawing of the decapitated Sloane Matthews. What had triggered my automatic drawing at the restaurant?

From experience, my gift was never random. Somehow, that place or the people in it had a connection to Sloane—could it be the bartender with the bad vibe? I reached into my purse to retrieve the drawing—shit. It wasn't there. I was certain I'd grabbed it, but in my haste to leave, I must've dropped it.

Another mistake, Evelyn.

I pulled out my paper and pencil, re-sketched the drawing from memory, and jotted down the clairaudient number—117.

What clue did the number hold?

Had there been a development in Leo's case? Was the

number related to that? If my drawing and numerical message would help Leo, I should call him or Parker and—

Stop. Leo had made it clear he didn't want me to contact Parker or have anything to do with his investigations. If I was going to keep him, I couldn't cross his boundaries—again. I had to solve the mystery on my own. I was close. I felt it in my bones. My sixth sense had led me here, and I knew I was closing in on something.

I took a cleansing breath and called out to the universe to give me a sign.

Then I tore open a bag of chips and crunched down the salty snacks as I mindlessly flipped through the brochures. There was a water park featuring giant dinosaurs, a fireworks factory outlet, a zoo, a classic car museum…

All the amusements were touristy until I came across one that advertised: "A nature getaway and relaxation center nestled on the homestead of a five-hundred-acre working farm."

The hotel and day spa advertised hiking trails, a farm-to-table restaurant, animal enrichment programs, guided horseback riding trails, falconry, a meditation center, a yoga studio, chakra cleansing massage…

My personal Nirvana.

Mentally, I was torched. I needed a break from the stress just as much as Leo. Maybe I'd check into the paradise that Livingston Farm promised while I worked on solving the mystery? I wasn't taking care of myself and needed to nourish my body and mind with positive energy.

Riding a horse on a trail and immersing myself in nature would help clear my mind. I needed to focus on my goals for the future while giving Leo the space to acclimate to his new life.

Just because Leo asked me not to leave, that didn't mean he wanted me back. He had crossed the line when he berated me about my gift, but Leo had experienced a traumatic event, and I knew that part of that was venting his frustrations on me.

He apologized, and I forgave him. But I had to admit that Leo bringing Rochelle into our home crushed me. If I lived a thousand years, I would never unsee that. And then there was his insinuation that he was better off before he'd met me. Downright brutal.

I tossed the chips into the trash, unable to stomach any more garbage.

I missed Leo so badly. All I wanted was to go home, wrap my arms around him, and make him understand how much I love him. Even though his memory had vanished, Leo had to feel something for me.

Stick to the plan, Evelyn. Leo needs time to heal.

I had to stop Vaughn's premonition from coming to pass. The only way to do that was to find Aurora. My instincts had led me to the restaurant in Grandview, and now this brochure was offering me a fairytale farm out in the middle of the woods—just like the setting of my dreams.

I flipped through the brochure again. The resort was off the highway at exit 117—the numeric clue I received at the restaurant. I no longer had any doubts about where I was going or what I needed to do.

I know I'll find the answer there. Trust your instincts, Evelyn.

If I left now, I would reach my destination in an hour.

Livingston Farm, here I come.

FOCUS—LEO

I made it to Grandview in record time.

Evelyn's map led me to this exit, but I had no clue where to find her. I did some quick calculations to come up with an educated guess of why she might have pulled over here.

As far as we could tell, Evelyn had no knowledge that she had drawn a roadmap. So, that meant she had pulled off the highway for a reason. She was probably hungry and needed to fill up the car with gas.

She could accomplish both goals here. There were a couple of fast-food chains, but Evelyn wasn't a burger and fries kind of person. Where would Evelyn go for lunch?

I followed the main road and drove through a quaint downtown area that Evelyn would've loved to explore. There were antique stores, an old-fashioned style ice cream parlor, a neighborhood bar, and a family-owned restaurant.

Since I had zero to go on, I parked the car and started walking. Duke was tired from a long day of travel, but he perked up and was ready for another mission the moment his paws hit the pavement.

His nose was down, and he started sniffing with a purpose.

"Need a nice patch of grass, buddy?"

There was a small common area between buildings just ahead, but as I steered him in that direction, he resisted and stayed on course.

"Come on, Duke." I tugged on his lead, but the dog held his ground and was determined to stay on the sidewalk. As the dog plowed ahead with his nose down and his tail high, I came up with a crazy idea—what if Duke is tracking Evelyn?

Her scent was fresh. He was a trained search and rescue dog. It was a stretch, but considering I had tracked her this far using "paranormal phenomena," it wasn't out of the realm of possibility that Duke had picked up her scent.

I lifted one of Evelyn's drawings out of my jacket and held it out for the dog to sniff. Since I had nothing to lose, I gave him a command. "Search."

Duke wagged his tail as he headed down the sidewalk. When we reached the restaurant, the dog circled a menu board in front of the door. I glanced at the day's offerings and noted the special dessert was pumpkin cheesecake—something Evelyn would've loved.

Before I thought too hard about it, Duke sniffed the door handle and sat at attention, signaling he had located his target.

"Good boy." I patted the dog on the head and went inside. A hostess greeted me and smiled at the dog. Duke was wearing his K9 harness and was welcome in the restaurant as a service animal. "Just the two of you today?"

I scanned the restaurant in search of Evelyn. "Actually, I'm looking for someone." I pulled a photo of Evelyn out of my jacket and handed it to the young lady. "Has she been in today?"

The hostess studied the smiling photo of her and then

shrugged. "I'm not sure. There was a lady in her twenties here earlier, but I can't say for certain it was her."

"Can I help you?" A gray-haired woman who appeared to be in charge came forward. She had a black apron tied around her waist, and her back was slightly hunched, probably from years of carrying heavy trays.

I repeated my question and handed her the photo.

She put on a pair of glasses and studied Evelyn's face. She lowered the photo and shifted her gaze between me and the dog. "Are you a cop?"

"Detective Leo Ricci, Violent Crimes Task Force." I handed her my business card to prove my identity. It was a good sign that the woman wanted to confirm my identity before giving me information.

"Is she in trouble?" the woman asked.

"She has committed no crimes. Her family is concerned about her, and I'm following up on a safety check."

"A woman came in dressed in black with a baseball cap and sunglasses on. She could be the woman you're looking for, but I can't say for certain." She pointed to a guy behind the bar. "Go talk to Dillon. He struck up a conversation with her."

I moved to the bar to question the witness.

"Yeah, she was here. I talked to her a bit. I offered her a drink—on the house—but she didn't want it."

Damn right. My girlfriend would never accept a drink from a stranger.

"How was her demeanor? Did she seem okay?"

The bartender wiped the spots off a wine glass as he considered my question. "She looked nervous, like she was afraid someone would recognize her. She had on a ball cap and sunglasses. I don't know what she was worried about, but she left without eating the mac and cheese she ordered."

I choked back a rush of guilt. Evelyn had left home

because of me, and if Dr. Vaughn was right, she was chasing someone or something. Was Evelyn trying to stay incognito because she was tracking Nolan?

Was this her way of proving to me that her paranormal gift was real?

The fact that Nolan Bradford had visited her gallery meant that he was either following me, or he had intended to hurt Evelyn to settle his vendetta against me. Evelyn may've deciphered a clue we hadn't put together yet and had gone rogue to track down an alleged killer.

"What else can you tell me about her? Any information might help me track her down."

"Well, she did something strange," the guy said. "I thought she was really hot and was going to ask her out, but after I saw her drawing—"

"What did she draw?"

"I mean, like, it was some really twisted shit, man. On the verge of psycho-killer kind of art. She drew a gory picture of a decapitated lady ghost oozing with blood right here in the bar. It was sick as hell, but really fucking cool, you know?"

Christ. Why would she draw that in public?

"What did she do with the art? Did you get a good look at it?"

"Yeah. I have it. I found it on the floor near her table. When she bolted, I went over to get a closer look. It was too cool to throw away, so I kept it." He reached behind the counter and set a water-stained sketch on the bar. She'd drawn it on the back of a paper placemat.

The bartender was right—it was a psycho-killer brand of art.

"I need to take this as evidence. Did you take any photos?"

"No." The bartender shook his head and then dropped his gaze to the bar.

He was lying. "Let me see your phone," I said.

Dillon wrinkled his brow as he considered how to respond. He lifted his phone from his pocket. "Like I said, she was really hot, man. I didn't mean to spook her. I just wanted her picture because she was pretty." He turned the phone so I could see the picture.

Evelyn's gaze was fixed out the window, watching the rain. Her expression was heavy with sadness, and I wished I had the power to jump into that moment and pull her out of her unloved and underappreciated state of mind.

I deleted the photo and handed the guy back his phone. I resisted the urge to lecture the little prick about taking photos of women behind their backs, but trying to explain why it was wrong would be a waste of breath.

Instead, I remained professional to keep him talking. "Thank you for your help, Dillon. Anything else I should know?"

"Yeah. I noticed something really bizarre in the background." The bartender pointed to a shadowy figure at the edge of the drawing.

I leaned in for a closer look. She'd drawn this very bar, right here in this restaurant. On the left side of the drawing, the shadowy figure was—shit, it was Nolan Bradford. What the hell?

"Do you recognize him?" I pointed to the professor.

"Yeah, that's Max. He was a regular here for a while. He took off one day, and we never saw him again."

I brought up a picture of Nolan Bradford on my phone. "This is Max? Did you see him here today?"

"Yes, that's him. No, he wasn't here. That's so fucking weird, right?"

You have no idea, buddy.

Going on a hunch, I showed the bartender a photo of Cora Bradford. "What about her? Have you ever seen her before?"

Dillon studied the photo of the professor's wife. She had short brown hair and was of average build and height. No distinguishing characteristics that made her stand out from the crowd.

"I mean, she might be the lady who came in with him one day, but if it's her, she looks really different now."

"What can you tell me about her?"

"Well, Max always came in alone, but one day a lady came in and kind of surprised him. Once he saw her, he paid his check and left. They argued on the sidewalk for a minute, and then they were gone. That's why I remember. I thought Max was a loner."

"Did they leave together?" I asked.

"Not sure, man. I didn't see them leave."

I was new to this paranormal thing, but Evelyn must've had some vision or insight that led her here. My team had zero leads on Cora and Nolan's whereabouts. But the big picture was coming into focus. Evelyn was on a mission to find Nolan and possibly Cora Bradford.

Even though it was dangerous, reckless, and way beyond her scope as an artist, my psychic/medium girlfriend was playing junior detective and tracking down the suspects in my assault—and persons of interest in the Sloane Matthews case.

Evelyn was in serious danger now. I needed to find her before she got herself into a situation where she didn't have the skills or training to survive.

HUNTING—LEO

The investigation was moving in the right direction —thanks to Evelyn. I had a positive ID and last known location on Nolan Bradford, which gave Parker a reason to follow the case to Grandview.

I was still on medical leave and wasn't actively involved in the investigation, but I trusted my team to track down the suspect. My main concern now was finding Evelyn and bringing her home safely.

After working with Parker and finding the hidden clues in her art, I was becoming a believer in this paranormal thing. The eerie details in Evelyn's drawings were steering us toward new leads in the case, making it nearly impossible for me to write it off as a coincidence.

While I considered the gravity of Evelyn's gift, it was the dog who helped me understand that not everything in life could be easily explained. How was it possible that Duke used his sense of smell and training to track down Evelyn? K9s have been working with law enforcement to track people for centuries.

Working animals have senses far more developed than our own, but we trust their instincts and follow their leads. Why then was it so hard for me to believe that Evelyn had an elevated sixth sense that gave her a glimpse into the afterlife?

While Parker and the FBI followed up on the Nolan Bradford lead, Duke and I hit the road once again. I got off at the next exit on Evelyn's map and went into a couple of businesses until I scored a hit. When I flashed her picture in a big box chain store, one cashier remembered selling Evelyn a cheap cell phone.

This was a relief because it meant that Evelyn was okay, and hopefully, she had purchased the phone to contact me. It also validated that the markers on the map would lead me to Evelyn.

The next star on the map was only an hour away. While I was eager to see Evelyn, my detective's brain was concerned about something the bartender had said.

Evelyn got spooked and left the restaurant without eating. Why? Had she seen Nolan? Maybe she was closer to finding him than I believed. Just because the bartender hadn't seen him, that didn't mean he wasn't there. But if Evelyn was that close, why the hell didn't she contact me or Parker?

Because you told her not to, remember?

I'd made it clear I didn't want her involved in my cases. No more drawings, no more amateur sleuthing, and no more contacting my partner with make-believe leads about my crime scenes.

Fuck. Evelyn left her phone in Chicago because she didn't want me to track her down and stop her from hunting a dangerous man. I had already concluded that Evelyn believed the only way to win me back was to prove her gift was real by tracking down Nolan Fucking Bradford.

Dammit. If Evelyn was half the determined woman my mom had described, she would go to any lengths necessary to save our relationship.

AURORA—EVELYN

$\mathcal{W}$elcome to Livingston Farm!

I had bought a burner phone and called ahead to make a reservation. The single rooms inside the main lodge had all been booked for the weekend, but they had an unoccupied suite in one of the historic homes available.

When I pulled into the entrance, I suddenly had misgivings. The resort was surrounded by farmland and nestled in the woods—just like the setting in my nightmare. The one with horrible things chasing me and that eerie female ghost and the old graveyard. And here I was, chasing them back.

Leo would lose his mind if he knew what I was up to. But I had come this far and wasn't about to turn back now. One of my clairaudient messages led me straight to this place.

When I entered the welcome lodge, the lobby bar was hopping with hipsters and nature lovers enjoying craft cocktails and bar snacks, while a shaggy-haired musician strummed a guitar and sang a John Denver classic.

"The staff is freshening up your suite. We haven't had

visitors stay there for a while, so it needed a quick touch-up. Would you like to have a drink at the bar while you wait?"

Now that I was here, I might as well enjoy myself. "A drink sounds amazing."

I ordered the house special—a citrus and honey-infused bourbon on the rocks. I sat in a rocking chair by the fireplace and sipped my cocktail as the crowd sang along to Rocky Mountain High.

While the alcohol and ambience of the lodge melted my tension away, I reminded myself that life was a series of highs and lows. I had faced many challenges in my life and bounced back every time—stronger than I was before.

As I relaxed by the fire, I admired the rustic décor. There was a watercolor rendering of the farm by a local artist, vintage photos of the original owners, a cowbell on the shelf, beeswax candles—a vintage doll preserved in a case.

I snapped out of my loose and relaxed state of mind and hopped out of the chair. I moved to the shelf and studied the details of the doll. The pattern on her dress looked familiar, and I realized she resembled one of the dolls in my sketch.

I flagged down a server and inquired about the antique.

"Oh, she's one of many dolls you'll see around the lodge."

"Really?" I tried to level my excitement, but I was stunned by how close I was now to deciphering the doll clue. Well done, instincts. "What's the significance of the dolls?"

"Oh, they all belonged to one of the original owners of the farm—Mrs. Aurora Livingston."

Aurora.

The server pointed to a sepia-toned family photo on the wall of a mysterious woman in a long black dress with haunting dark eyes—the woman from my painting. My pulse raced as I stared at the photo taken in front of a small 1900-era farmhouse.

Aurora stood beside her husband and held a small child in

her arms—but this wasn't a happy picture. Aurora's eyes were dark and deep-set with a mournful expression.

As I studied the details, I realized the child was not real—it was a doll like the ones I had sketched in my automatic drawings. "Aurora sure loved her dolls," I said.

"Yeah, something like that." The server gave me a wry smile and handed me a brochure. "This is a brief history of the Livingston family. You should take a tour of the original farmhouse while you're here."

I clutched the paper as if it were a deed to the heavens, as a rush of excitement flooded over me. I was zeroing in on the clues that would help solve the case—and help me get the love of my life back.

HOPE—EVELYN

When my suite was ready, a member of the staff escorted me to my room and gave me a brief tour of the house where I was staying.

The furniture was a mix of modern and period pieces, and the décor appeared to be paintings and collectibles from the original owners.

As the friendly staffer, Charlie, led me upstairs, the temperature in the house dropped about ten degrees. A mournful feeling rushed over me, and my heart was heavy with heartache and hopelessness.

Charlie hesitated before opening the door to my suite. "Some guests find this room unsettling."

"Unsettling how?" I asked.

Charlie shrugged and led me inside.

Holy crap. The room was filled with dozens of vintage dolls.

"Aurora loved and cherished each doll in this room. She had given birth to five children during her marriage, but they all passed away in childhood."

"That's tragic," I said.

"Her hopes of having more children were dashed when her husband died, leaving her to live out her days as a childless widow."

I scanned the room and studied the antique faces. The dolls' heads were made from a hard, composite material with hand-painted features and glass eyes. There were small cracks and discolored spots on their faces, and the hair varied in color and texture, leading me to believe it was human hair.

The dolls' bodies were all soft, and based on their age, likely stuffed with straw. I imagined Aurora hand-stitching their little bodies and making their clothes from fabric scraps and burlap potato sacks.

"These dolls became Aurora's pretend family after she was forced to live out her life in solitude. When she died, she willed the entire estate to her children and hired a staff to care for them until the money ran out and the home eventually sold at auction."

"That's a sad story. So, this was Aurora's house?"

"Yes, she lived here with her husband. When he passed away, she packed up all the dolls and moved into a smaller house at the edge of the property. But this room was Aurora's nursery. It's kind of sad, right?"

I nodded in agreement. "Yeah, for sure. Aurora wanted a big family but ended up alone. Tragic."

Charlie smiled sympathetically. "I'm afraid we are completely booked, so I don't have another room for you, but I have you scheduled with your resort coordinator, Angela, in the morning," he said.

"She will help you book your agenda and make sure your stay is perfect. I'll give her a heads up that if anything else comes available, she can snag new accommodations for you."

This room looked like a movie set for a D-list horror

flick. But I was here to track down clues and solve the mystery. "No worries, the dolls are beautiful."

My goal was to find out who had attacked Leo. These dolls and Aurora were somehow related to the case. Nothing —not even an army of creepy Victorian dolls—would keep me from solving the mystery.

I spent the rest of the day researching the Livingston family history. My first task was to find a link between the past and the present. That was harder than it seemed. Once I had exhausted my efforts, I settled in for the evening.

My brains cells had fizzled out, and I needed rest before continuing my quest. I snuggled under the covers, closed my eyes, and drifted off to sleep.

"WHAAA, WHAAA, WHAAA…"

The sound of a baby crying woke me from a deep sleep. I sat up and found a mother soothing her child in the rocking chair beside my bed. When the woman noticed I was there, she smiled and pressed a finger to her lips. "Shhh…"

I gave her a nod, acknowledging her request. From my bed, I watched the tender moment play out before me. The room was dark, but a beam of moonlight shined in through the window.

When my eyes adjusted and I could see more clearly, I noticed the mother's skin was pale blue, her lips were black, and her cheeks were sallow. Her skin had melted away in places, revealing her bones, and wild tufts of gray hair sprouted from her ears.

With bony hands, the mother unbuttoned her blouse and peeled one sleeve over her shoulder, then pressed the child to her bosom to breastfeed it.

Oh, God. Her chest was sunken in and oozing with decay. Clearly, the mother was no longer among the living. As I studied her dark lace clothing and the style of her hair, I recognized her as the woman I'd seen in the vintage photos at the lodge—Aurora Livingston.

This is a dream.

Unable to escape my nightmare, I glanced down at the baby and prepared to see a horrendous sight I could never unsee, but when I looked more closely, I realized the child was a doll.

The disillusioned mother ghost was treating the toy as if it were her own flesh and blood. As I watched her caring for her baby doll, something flew past me and smacked the wall above my bed, then landed next to me. I picked it up and saw a crack on her forehead from the force of the blow.

The ghostly mother floated out of her chair and hissed at the horror of seeing one of her children damaged. She shot a vengeful gaze around the room, searching for the perpetrator of the crime.

The room was empty aside from us.

The mother picked up the doll and clutched it protectively.

Wham! Wham! Wham!

Dolls after doll after doll flew around the room, crashing into furniture and banging against the walls. I couldn't see who was committing the senseless act of violence, but the ghostly mother spun around in a tailspin, trying in vain to protect her precious family.

When she couldn't find the source, she turned her attention to me. The angry ghost whipped her head in my direction and stormed to my bedside. She clawed at me with her decayed hands, hissing and snarling. Her mouth twisted as she tried to speak, but her withered black tongue wiggled in her mouth like an oily black eel.

Wake up, Evelyn. Wake up!

As I covered my hands over my head to protect myself, a

loud chopping noise outside my window woke me from my nightmare.

I slid out of bed and put my hands on my knees as I caught my breath. I glanced out the window and realized it was morning now. In the sunlight, I noticed a woman wearing denim overalls chopping firewood. As I watched her swing the axe, a single word popped into my head.

Hope.

TROUBLE—LEO

According to the map, I would find Evelyn at the next exit.

It had been easy to track her down at the first stop, thanks to my K9. The second location was easy, too, because I got lucky and hit the right place in only a few tries.

The next location would be trickier because there wasn't much there.

When I veered off the highway, there were no businesses in sight. As I sat at the flashing yellow light, a sign pointed to Williamsville in one direction and Hartman Hills in the other.

The road was a two-lane highway flanked by farmland. There were no hotels, restaurants, or even a gas station at this exit. It was one of those necessary off-ramps for the townspeople, but the population was too small and far from civilization for businesses.

I pulled off the highway and walked Duke as I studied the map.

Why did you lead me here, Evelyn?

The map had led me to her twice so far, but my gut was telling me something wasn't right.

I still hadn't figured out the significance of the word Aurora. Since Evelyn and Vaughn had independently come up with the word, I surmised the clue wasn't random. Just as I was typing the word into my phone, my cell buzzed with a call from my partner.

"Hey, Parker. Any leads on Nolan?"

"The bartender was very helpful, but we haven't tracked down our suspect yet. I have the team following up on new leads now. Where are you?"

I updated him on my location.

"I'm not far behind. Want to meet up?"

I could use a second opinion and agreed to wait for him at the exit. When he arrived, we studied Evelyn's map. We had hit a wall with the current location, so we concentrated on the next location.

Exit 117.

We agreed the Aurora clue was the key to finding Evelyn. I typed the word along with the exit into my search.

"Our founders, Henry and Aurora, settled the Livingston Farm…"

"Got it. I found a website about the property. It's an hour away. Evelyn is there, I know it."

"Good work, partner. Want me to come with you?" Parker asked.

"No. I need to do this alone. Focus on finding Nolan and Cora, and I'll see to it Evelyn is safe." As I was about to leave, I remembered Duke was due to go back to his handler the next morning. "Can you take Duke back with you? Jenna will lose her mind if I don't have her dog waiting to greet her when she gets back from her honeymoon."

Parker was happy to have a companion on his drive back to the city. Even though I had only been with the K9 for a short time, I had grown attached to the hardworking and loyal dog.

I patted him on the head and praised him for helping me find Evelyn before I hit the road to make amends with the woman I planned to spend the rest of my life with.

As adrenaline pumped through my veins, I imagined how Evelyn would react when she saw me. She had gone to a lot of trouble to elude me. What if our reunion wasn't a happy one?

If I was being honest with myself, her safety was my number one concern, but I missed her. My drive to hunt her down wasn't only because I wanted to protect her from an encounter with Nolan, or because I needed to apologize face to face. I wanted to see Evelyn because I longed to be with her.

There was something about Evelyn that lured me to her. From the moment she disappeared, all I could think about was getting her back. Yes, life with Evelyn had its complications. Her gift was a strange and dangerous phenomenon that I was only beginning to understand.

But no matter how difficult my future would be with the alluring artist, every instinct in my body led me back to her. I was ready to face the challenges ahead and be the brave and supportive man an incredible woman like Evelyn deserved.

As I sped down the highway, an unsettling thought entered my mind. What if she changed her mind and didn't want to be with me?

SOLO—EVELYN

The lodge buzzed with excitement as guests filled their plates from the farm-to-table breakfast buffet and dined al fresco on the patio.

While I sipped a cappuccino and noshed on a sampling of fresh-baked goodies, a woman wearing a forest green Livingston Farm t-shirt approached. "You must be Lauren. I'm Angela, your resort coordinator here at the Livingston Farm."

When I checked in, I'd used my birth name. It would be a stretch for someone to recognize me from my gallery in Chicago, but I wanted to stay incognito while I was playing junior detective.

"Nice to meet you, Angela. Please, join me." I motioned to the empty chair across from me.

"How did you sleep last night?" Angela tucked her long auburn hair behind her ears and gave me all her attention. Her big brown eyes shined, and her sun-kissed skin radiated a healthy glow.

The farm boasted about the medicinal quality of home-made food and how the positive effects of being in nature nourished our mind, body, and soul. Seeing the staff in picture-perfect health gave me hope I could rebound from my tumultuous life and get back to my positive state of mind.

"Perfect. The room is lovely."

Angela suppressed a giggle and eyed me suspiciously. She leaned in as if to tell me a secret. "Guests have run out of that room in the middle of the night. Those old dolls have creeped everyone out who has ever stepped foot in there. I've spoken to the front desk, and we're trying to find new accommodations for you."

"You're sweet for trying, but really, the room is fine. The dolls aren't creepy to me. I think they're beautiful."

"Of course they are." Angela cackled more robustly than I would've expected. She tossed back her head and closed her eyes as if my statement about the dolls was the funniest thing she had ever heard.

It seemed an over-the-top reaction considering the tragic story attached to the dolls—even a touch disrespectful to the founding family members.

"If you're happy, I'm happy," Angela said as her smile faded. "Now, let's talk about your schedule. What are you in the mood for today? A guided walking tour, spa day, paddle boarding, hot yoga, falconry…"

"Are you offering the guided horseback riding tour today?" I asked hopefully.

"We have a group leaving after breakfast. You'll ride for a couple of hours, then stop for lunch at the picnic grove. Shall I sign you up solo, or will your boyfriend be joining you?"

"Boyfriend?"

"Oh, sorry if that was foreword of me to assume. I figured you must be here with someone, and there's no ring on your finger." She scrunched her face apologetically—another strange reaction.

"No problem. I'm here alone."

"Perfect." Angela tapped the reservation on her phone. "Now, let's talk about the rest of your weekend plans."

Angela had thrown me off when she asked about my boyfriend. Part of me was glad Leo was taking some time to rest and recharge after his trauma. But the side of me who longed to be with him secretly hoped he would use his detective skills to track me down.

WISHFUL THINKING, Evelyn. Leo is probably relieved you left town for a few days.

CONNECTION—LEO

I entered the welcome lodge, identified myself as a detective, and flashed Evelyn's photo at the front desk.

The two employees studied the picture. "That looks like someone who was here earlier," one said to the other. "The woman who just left for the horseback riding tour."

"Are you sure?" I asked.

The other one nodded in agreement. "Super nice and really excited to meet the horses." She tapped on her keyboard and brought up an event schedule. "What is her name?"

"Evelyn Sinclair."

She shook her head. "Oh, shoot. Sorry, no one is here by that name."

"Try Lauren Murphy." Evelyn may have checked in using an alias, and I knew her birth name from the articles about her near drowning. She had changed her name years ago when she started a new life as an artist. It was a good place to start.

"Yes, Lauren is here! She loves animals, apparently. She

signed up for goat yoga, falconry, and a paddleboat ride on the duck pond followed by lunch with llamas."

I was relieved that Evelyn had come here to relax and have some time to recuperate after our argument. I'd learned she grew up in a small town in Ohio and loved being around animals and nature. "Where can I find her?"

"The only way to catch up with the group is on horse-back. Do you want me to call ahead to the barn and have them saddle up a ride for you?"

Anything for you, Evelyn.

BY THE TIME my horseback riding guide and I had caught up to Evelyn's group, they had stopped by the lake to rest and take photos of the beautiful scenery. Everyone was scattered, doing their own thing.

I scanned the crowd and couldn't find Evelyn among the other riders. I stayed on the horse and went around the bend —there you are, beautiful. Evelyn was alone, walking a brown horse along the water's edge.

She spoke softly to the animal and stroked its neck as if sharing her deepest secrets with a trusted friend. Evelyn appeared calm and happy in her natural element, enjoying a private moment with her riding companion.

Everything I'd been feeling since my attack whipped around in my head like a boomerang. One minute, I felt a rush of excitement stemming from our intimate moment in our bedroom.

Then I felt the nagging jab of betrayal and mistrust when Evelyn failed to be honest with me. The shock of seeing the drawings of my crime scenes and how she'd gone behind my back to discuss my case with my partner.

But all those negative feelings were swept away when, at last, I'd found her safe. Whatever I was feeling, relief, joy, love…all I knew was that nothing else mattered now that Evelyn and I were together again.

Finally, I let go of anger about losing my memory and focused on the calm and quiet beauty guiding her horse to graze in the tall grass growing along the creek bed. I didn't want to spook her by calling her name or steal her joy by showing up at her special place unannounced, but I was here now and couldn't wait another moment to reunite with her.

I dismounted the horse, clutched the reins, and led the animal to her. When Evelyn heard us approaching, she looked up to see who joined her. When she realized it was me, she stared in bewilderment.

I was sure a million things were going through her mind. Her expression remained in a state of shock as she processed what I was doing there, how I'd found her, or why I'd tracked her down.

Would she feel violated because I used my detective skills to find her?

As she stood there, processing her emotions, a warm smile crept up on her lips as she formed her theory. "Leo, you got your memory back!" She ran to me and wrapped her arms around my body as if she would never let me go again.

I stroked her hair and rocked her as the relief of seeing Evelyn safe was an answered prayer. Her warm body melted into mine, and we embraced as if we had been separated for a lifetime.

"I was so scared. I thought I lost you forever." She peeked up at me as she choked back tears. "You stopped loving me, Leo. You thought I was lying about my gift. You shattered my heart, babe. I had to leave. I couldn't be around you anymore knowing how you felt about me."

Damn. Now I had to break her heart all over again when I told her that whole year was still lost to me. "Everything's okay now. I'm here."

"When did it happen? Did all your memories come back at once?"

I kissed her on top of the head, then pulled back to meet her eyes. "I'm here because I was worried about you. I didn't like how we left things, and I wanted to make things right between us."

Evelyn's elation tanked. "But you did get your memory back, right?" Her teary eyes glistened hopefully in the sunshine as she awaited my answer.

As I held Evelyn in my arms, I felt vulnerable in a way that went against my strong-willed, independent grain. She deserved an honest answer, but the last thing I wanted to do after I'd gone to great lengths to find her was shatter her heart again.

"When you left, I felt empty. I'm taking that as a sign a part of me is still holding on to you, Evelyn."

She stared into my eyes, waiting for another bomb to drop.

"What I'm trying to say is, I don't want to give up on us. I may not remember the past, but I feel a connection to you I can't explain."

At last, Evelyn's expression softened. "I'll never give up on us, Detective. Thank you for finding me. I love you." She rested her head on my chest and squeezed her arms around me.

We still had a lot to talk about, but the most important thing in my life right now was getting my personal life in order. I had confidence in Parker and our team to track down Nolan and would use my downtime to work toward a new normal.

"I'll ask the guide to lead us back to the barn, and from there, we can go back to the lodge. I know horseback riding isn't your thing—"

"Not a chance," I said. "I love horses. No way am I leaving

early." I gave Evelyn an ornery grin. I was a city guy, and while I had a lot of respect for cowboys, I was far from comfortable in the saddle. But if horses made Evelyn happy, I would do anything to keep that beautiful smile on her face.

"You don't have to suffer because of me," Evelyn teased. "We can go back."

I picked up her hand and kissed the inside of her wrist. "I'm looking forward to spending time with you, Evelyn. I want to fall in love with you all over again."

I don't know where that came from, but those were the most honest words I had ever spoken.

DIRTY—EVELYN

 $\mathcal{B}$ utterflies of excitement fluttered in my stomach as I replayed Leo's romantic words.

I want to fall in love with you all over again.

While he had insisted he wanted to finish the horseback riding tour, all I wanted to do was burrow into his arms and talk about all that had gone down over the last few days.

The only way he could've tracked me down was through Vaughn—but I'd never told him who I was going to visit. Leo had to have found out about Aurora. He was a top-notch detective, but finding my location with only a single word to guide him seemed impossible.

What other clues had he used to track me down way out here?

After about an hour on the trail, we reached the picnic grove where we were set up to have lunch. I wanted to spend time alone with Leo, so I asked a member of the maintenance crew if we could catch a lift back to the lodge. She was happy to give us a ride in the back of her pickup truck.

When we reached the reception area, a front desk staff

member approached with a big smile. "I see you found your friend."

"Yes, thank you for sending him to me."

The perky staff member blushed as she snuck glances at my handsome boyfriend. "I spoke to your activity guide, Angela, and she found another room."

"Fantastic," I said.

"It's at the farthest end of the property and has three bedrooms, a fire pit, and a hot tub in the primary suite. It's super private and off the beaten path, so we provide a golf cart for transportation, along with a fully stocked bar, and a private dining option if you don't want to leave your room."

A private cabin nestled in the woods during the most beautiful season of the year. Being alone in paradise gave me hope that the universe was finally giving me a break from all the misfortune.

"Sounds like heaven." I smiled at Leo.

"We'll take it," he said.

"Give us an hour to get it all set up. In the meantime, help yourself to the s'mores station out back at the firepit."

"Perfect. Please thank Angela for us."

GRAVEL CRUNCHED under the wheels of the golf cart as we pulled up the driveway to our private log cabin. The scent of burning firewood greeted us as we walked along the stone-paved sidewalk that led to a covered front porch.

There was a pair of rocking chairs and a large, vertical sign with hand-painted letters that announced, Welcome, Ya'll!

When Leo unlocked the front door and led us inside, I beamed at the rustic charm and farmhouse chic décor of our quaint accommodations. The furniture was an eclectic mix of antiques and modern wood furniture with fun, farm-themed accessories.

There was a basket made of chicken wire on the kitchen counter, loaded with fresh fruit, and a wooden cutting board next to it carved in the shape of a cow.

Leo grinned as I beamed at the fun and whimsical barn-yard-themed pillows, throw blankets, and accessories. Then he took my hand and led us into the bedroom.

The vibe of this room was way different than the cutesy farmhouse living room. The canopy bed was covered with a frilly red satin bedspread and heart-shaped pillows.

There was a bottle of champagne on ice on the night-stand, along with a selection of chocolate truffles and juicy strawberries. Romantic instrumental music played in the background, and the aromatic scent of roses wafted around the room.

"Now we're getting to the good part." Leo took my hand and led me into the spacious bathroom, where a bubble bath was ready for our arrival. Rose petals floated on the surface of the warm, steamy water, and the fresh scent of eucalyptus and pine filled the air.

Leo held my hand and drew my body close to his. "You look a little dirty, Evelyn. I better get you cleaned up."

I cracked up at Leo's not-so-subtle hint about how he wanted to kick off our romantic weekend. The thought of sinking into the warm, sudsy bath with my studly boyfriend gave me a rush of excitement.

We had made love the first night Leo was home from the hospital. It was a quickie, and the room was dark, and I hadn't yet comprehended the gravity of Leo's memory loss. This time, however, it felt like make-up sex.

We'd never been down this road together before, and I was ready to start fresh with Leo. I slid my fingers along the waist of his belt and gave the leather a little tug. My simple, sexy gesture caused a groan to escape his lips.

I knew what Leo liked and had a million ways to please my sexy boyfriend. "I could get a little dirtier before you clean me up, Detective."

Leo lifted an eyebrow, intrigued by my naughty joke.

Finally, Leo and I were on the same page.

LIFETIME—LEO

I popped the champagne and poured a round of bubbly as I waited for Evelyn to slip into something sexy.

Knowing she was excited to give our relationship a fresh start made me grateful beyond measure—but I still couldn't shake the nagging question.

Why did she run away from me?

If she loved me as much as she claimed, why had she gone to such extremes to make certain I wouldn't find her?

The bathroom door creaked open. Evelyn emerged in the doorway wearing only a pair of lace panties. Her long, wavy hair spilled over her shoulders and covered her perky breasts.

"God, Evelyn. You're gorgeous."

As she prowled toward the bed, my gaze drifted down her smoking-hot body, taking in the curve of her silhouette and toned, sexy legs.

Evelyn's lips curled into a smile as I picked up her hand and spun her around so I could admire all her luscious curves. I slid my hands down her thighs and massaged her ass. The sensation of her warm, soft skin and her sexy little groans of satisfaction sent all my blood south.

I kicked back the reasons Evelyn had been trying to hide from me and made room for all the dirty thoughts running through my mind about how I was going to please this gorgeous woman.

Evelyn pulled down my shorts, tossed them on the floor, and stroked me. She tugged gently, encouraging my growth, while rubbing her hardened nipples against my chest.

The anticipation of kissing her between the legs and tasting her sweet nectar excited me, and I couldn't wait to devour every inch of her body.

I pulled her into bed, guided her on her back, and slid off her underwear. I went down on her, swirling my tongue and sucking on her sweet spot as Evelyn dove her hands into my hair as her body reacted to my touch.

"God, Leo. You feel so good," Evelyn groaned.

Evelyn's breathing had gotten heavier as she panted on her way to climax. Her excitement made me rock hard, and the anticipation of her pleasure was driving me wild.

Evelyn's excitement piqued, and she let out an orgasmic exhale of satisfaction.

I ran my tongue across her V and savored her sweet release as I crawled up the bed and pressed my body on top of hers. I kissed her deeply as she wrapped her arms and legs around me, eager for me to push inside her.

"How do you want me to take you, beautiful?"

A sultry smile spread across her lips. "However you want me. I'm all yours, Detective."

Fuck. I wanted to dominate her. I felt the desire to flip her on her stomach, stack some pillows underneath her, and take her from behind.

I longed to thrust deep into her core and give it to her animal style, hard and fast. I imagined the sexual gratification of wrapping my arms around her taut waist and claiming her as her breasts bounced from the force and energy of our lovemaking.

As I played out the fantasy in my head, I massaged Evelyn's breasts and wondered if she'd ever let me slide between them. I imagined what it would feel like to be sandwiched between her bosom.

"I can read your mind, Leo." For a woman who had a paranormal gift, I wondered if she really could hear my sexy thoughts.

She took my hand and guided me to sit on the bench at the foot of the bed. She left for a moment and went to the bathroom to retrieve some massage oil. Evelyn locked her gaze on mine and squirted the oil over her chest.

Her skin glistened as she massaged herself, paying careful attention to her breasts.

"Fuck, Evelyn. You are the hottest woman on earth."

She tossed a heart-shaped pillow on the floor, dropped to her knees, and slid her tongue across my head. I sank my hands into her long, thick hair as she pleased me orally.

Watching her head bob as she brought me in and out of her mouth was the most satisfying act I had ever encountered. But when I had reached rock-hard status, she cupped her breasts and rubbed my cock between her oil-slicked breasts.

She peeked up at me as she rocked her body and massaged me in the most erotic way imaginable. I wouldn't last much longer and needed to be inside my sexy girlfriend. I grasped Evelyn's elbows and brought her to her feet.

I can bend her over the bed, sit her on my lap, position her on her knees...

As I considered my options, the most important part of our lovemaking was to be with her. I brought Evelyn to the bed and laid her gently on her back.

"You're an amazing woman, Evelyn." As I stared into her gorgeous blue eyes, I eased myself inside her. The sensation of our warm bodies syncing into a sensual rhythm was the greatest pleasure I had ever known.

I may not have remembered Evelyn from our past, but our bodies never lost touch. As we enjoyed our slow and sensual lovemaking, Evelyn's breathing got heavier as she headed toward climax.

"Take me there, Leo." She tapped me on the ass, encouraging me to make a run for the finish line. I stared into her eyes and followed my sexy girlfriend's command.

I kissed her deeply and savored her scent, her soft skin, and her sexy moans of satisfaction as we climaxed together. As we came down from our sexual high, I rolled on my side and cuddled her in my arms. "I love you, Evelyn."

"No, you don't," she teased.

"Maybe not today, but I will love you. All I want from you is a second chance. Promise you'll give me time to make our dreams come true."

Evelyn scratched her long nails gently down my back and drew the shape of a heart with her finger. "I'll give you a lifetime, Leo."

BETRAYAL—EVELYN

After a warm bath, Leo and I cuddled on the patio and sipped champagne as we came down from our romantic high.

The evening air was chilly, so I snuggled up to Leo as we sat under the stars and enjoyed our relaxing weekend getaway. I was a nature girl at heart and missed spending time in the great outdoors. We turned on the lanterns, lit candles, and added wood to the fire to illuminate our private space.

We hadn't yet discussed why I had run away from Chicago and covered my tracks so he couldn't find me. I also hadn't asked how he tracked me down. I didn't want to wreck our reunion by bringing up another paranormal matter he would undoubtedly not believe in.

As we listened to the owls hooting and the subtle sounds of the wind rustling the crunchy fall leaves, Leo was the first to break the awkward silence. "Are you curious about how I found you?"

I set down my champagne flute and turned to face him.

"Before we talk about that, I've made a decision about something that affects us both."

"Fine. You go first." Leo's complexion glowed from our late afternoon delight. I didn't want to ruin our moment by bringing up the forbidden subject, but he wanted us to have a future together, and I needed to be clear about my intentions.

While Leo and I wanted to be together, the problems that had torn us apart were still lurking in the shadows. Something had to change. There wasn't room in our relationship for Leo, me, and my ghosts.

I loved him more than anything on this earth, and losing him wasn't an option. When you love someone, you make sacrifices. The biggest threat to our relationship right now was me.

I stared at the flames and used the elemental energy of the fire to give me strength. "I've used my gift to take down killers and save lives. I've helped restless spirits find peace so they could move on to eternal bliss on the other side," I said.

"But every time I help a ghost, I put us in harm's way. And because of my gift, I almost lost the most important person in my life—you. I won't risk it again. I've paid my debt to the universe for giving me a second chance at life. No matter the consequences, I'm out of the ghost business."

I expected Leo to be thrilled I figured out a solution to save our relationship by denying my call of duty to the dead. But instead of cheering and wrapping his arms around me to celebrate, the calculated detective seemed skeptical.

"How can you stop using your gift? I thought you had no control over it."

"Correct. The only way I can think of to shut it off is to ignore the dreams and stop drawing. If I don't engage with the ghosts or act upon the messages I receive from the dead, maybe it will eventually stop."

"Have you tried it?"

"No, but trust me, babe. I won't give up. I promise I'll find a way to turn it off. You are more important to me than anything else in the entire world. I won't let my ghosts rob me of a life with the man I love."

As I spoke the words, I felt a sense of betrayal, like a dagger slicing through my heart. I didn't want to turn my back on the dead, but when my gift had nearly cost me my relationship with Leo, I had reached a fork in the road.

I couldn't have my ghosts and Leo, too. The decision was easy—I chose Leo.

THE CHOICE—LEO

That was the saddest thing I'd ever heard.

From what I'd learned about Evelyn, her gift was her identity. The cool and edgy artist of Halsted, who painted haunted places and ghostly beings, earned her a reputation as one badass ghost girl.

The idea that she was willing to scrap her identity and stop using her otherworldly talents to please me made me want to kick myself in the ass. Not only had I hurt her feelings, I had crushed her spirit to the point where she wanted to ditch her career and become a different person.

What did you expect, Ricci? You basically told her your life was better off before you met her.

Dammit. If there were a way to take back my selfish words, I'd shove them in a garbage bag, tie them to a cinder block, and chuck them into a watery grave. I never wanted to change Evelyn. Never meant to harm her or suggest that I couldn't love her because she had a talent I didn't understand.

What I needed to do was get ahead of this so she could salvage her self-worth and get back to being the incredible woman who would never let a shithead like me drag her down.

"That's a terrible idea," I said.

Evelyn lifted her eyebrows, surprised by my reaction. "Do you know a better way to solve the problem?"

"Yes, I do," I said. "Stop trying."

"What do you mean?"

"When I found your phone at the gallery, I checked your call log. I used the information to track you to Dr. Vaughn's place."

Evelyn's jaw dropped. "You went to Vaughn's house to track me down?"

"I did. When I told him I was concerned for your safety, he told me about Aurora."

Evelyn covered her mouth, likely floored that her friend had given me the sensitive information. "So, you tracked me here with a one-word clue?"

"Not entirely." I explained that I'd teamed up with Parker and determined her drawings had provided a roadmap that led me to the exits off the highway where she had gotten off.

I explained how her favorite K9, Duke, had led me to the restaurant where she had dined and how the bartender had confirmed she was there and even kept her creepy drawing.

"That's why you should never stop using your gift, Evelyn. There was a road map in your drawings that led me straight to you. Are you aware you sketched Nolan Bradford into your art?"

Evelyn shook her head in disbelief.

"I showed the bartender a photo of Nolan, and he confirmed seeing him—and possibly his wife Cora—at the restaurant. Parker and the FBI are now one step closer to finding the couple."

"That's incredible." Evelyn's complexion beamed as the

reality set in that she had single-handedly produced a lead in an otherwise stagnant investigation.

"Since the couple had been seen together, Parker believes they may have worked as a team to kill Sloane and cover up her murder. They both claimed to be home the night of her disappearance, providing each other with an alibi. Cora and Nolan Bradford are both persons of interest in Sloane's investigation and my assault case."

Evelyn was pacing the patio at this point. Her wheels were turning a mile a minute as she processed the information. "So, this means you believe me now?"

"I don't understand it all yet, but I know I was wrong when I accused you of lying. Your talent defies logic, but I promise I will do everything in my power to support you."

"My gift is dangerous," Evelyn said. "Communicating with the dead has nearly gotten us killed. You don't remember the times—"

"The past is behind us. The choice is yours, Evelyn. I'll support you no matter what you decide."

Evelyn stared into the woods as she pondered her decision. As long as I was a homicide detective, I would fight for justice. My life would always be in danger, but Evelyn was a civilian and had to decide what was best for her.

NIGHTMARE—EVELYN

What will I do if I dream of Sloane tonight?

Leo was resting peacefully beside me, but I'd been tossing and turning for hours. I slid out of bed and went into the kitchen for a glass of water.

While I sipped my drink, moonlight shined in from the window and illuminated the patio. The fire was still burning low, and I stared at the glowing embers to calm my mind.

As I thought about my future with Leo, a shadow darted past the window. Startled, I nearly spilled my water. It was the middle of the night. Who would be lurking around our cabin at this hour?

An animal, perhaps?

I hid behind the curtain and peeked into the darkness.

A beam of light flashed across the patio. I craned my neck to see around the corner, but from my vantage point, I only had access to a small section of the porch. I padded into the living room and drew back the curtain.

At that moment, someone aimed the flashlight at the window and caught me peeking through the curtain. I lifted my hand to shield my eyes from the bright light, and then, in a flash, the light was gone.

I heard the familiar sound of gravel crunching under tires and turned my attention toward the driveway. A golf cart was backing out, and I tried to make out the driver's face, but it was too dark outside.

Why is someone lurking around here at three o'clock in the morning?

Maybe someone was checking to make sure the fire was contained? Or someone wanted to clean up any leftovers or dirty dishes outside that would attract wild animals?

The retreat center was well-staffed, and it wasn't crazy to think employees were actively working all hours of the day. Let it go, Evelyn. I didn't want to wake Leo over nothing, so I got back into bed and tried to get some rest. As I listened to the familiar sound of my boyfriend's peaceful breathing, I drifted off to sleep.

CHOP...CHOP...CHOP...

I woke up in a panic. Someone was chopping wood outside our window. I reached over to wake Leo, but he wasn't there.

"Leo?" I called his name.

No answer.

I moved into the living room and opened the curtain to locate the source of the noise. Moonlight shined down on a tall male figure with an axe raised over his head. As I stared at the scene, the figure slammed the axe down onto a block of wood and severed the head off one of Aurora's dolls.

The head rolled onto the ground, and the doll's gaze fixated on mine. As I stared into its lifeless eyes, the man set another doll on the chopping block. He slammed down the axe and repeated the sequence until there was a pile of severed doll heads piled up on the ground.

Why is the man destroying Aurora's dolls?

The scene that played out was grainy, as if I was seeing the world through a sepia-toned filter. I heard a woman crying in the woods, but I couldn't see a face through the trees.

Footsteps padded toward me from inside the house.

"Leo?"

I turned and let out a blood-curdling scream when a ghostly woman dressed as Little Red Riding Hood crept up behind me and clutched my wrist.

"Get off me! Help!" I swung around and tried to wrestle out of her grasp, but she had a death grip on me, and I couldn't escape.

Blood oozed from her severed neck, and the noxious scent of burned flesh polluted the air. I screamed in vain as the ghost dragged me out of the house and into the woods, where the chopper was destroying Aurora's precious dolls.

When the ghost dragged me closer to the male figure in the woods, I realized he was dressed as the Big Bad Wolf— the counterpart to the ghostly, almost headless Little Red. He stopped chopping the dolls and pointed the axe at me as if choosing me as his next victim.

"Leave me alone! What do you want?"

As Little Red dragged me to the chopping block, I fought back with all the strength in my body. But I was unable to free myself. Red forced me to my knees and positioned my neck over the chopping block.

"This is a dream, Evelyn. Wake up! Wake up!"

Powerless to resist, the wolf raised the axe in ready position, and as the blade came down, I screamed a final plea for help.

A set of strong hands grasped my shoulders and called my name, pulling me out of my horrific nightmare.

THE DEAD—LEO

"I've got you, Evelyn. You're safe with me."

I smoothed her sweaty hair off her face and rubbed her back. "Just breathe. You had a nightmare. Everything is okay."

Evelyn panted as she recovered from what must've been a horrible dream. She touched her neck and darted her gaze around the floor, as if making sure whatever had frightened her was no longer in the room.

"Was this one of your ghost dreams?" I asked.

Evelyn hopped out of bed and moved to the back window. "Yes. I dreamed of Sloane Matthews again—but this time, someone new entered my dream. A man was there, decapitating dolls, and then he tried to chop my head off."

She got out of bed and paced the room. "Aurora was there, too. I couldn't see her, but I heard her crying."

"Wait. Did you just say, Aurora?"

Evelyn inhaled a deep breath to calm herself. "Yes. She's been visiting me in my dreams. The antique dolls in my sketches belong to her. She loved those things as if they were her own flesh and blood."

This paranormal gift of Evelyn's was remarkable. It was beyond my comprehension how she received these messages, but from what I experienced, her clairaudient clues were all on the mark.

"Tell me about the man with the axe. What do you remember about him?"

Evelyn lifted her eyes as she recalled her dream. "He was wearing a wolf mask."

Mentally, I took a step back and revisited the original crime scene a year ago. Sloane was last seen alive at the bonfire, wearing a Little Red Riding Hood costume. Her roommate said she had come to the party alone.

If Sloane dressed up as Red, who was the Big Bad Wolf?

An eyewitness had signed a sworn statement that she had seen Nolan Bradford's vehicle at the location that evening— but no one could confirm seeing Nolan in attendance at the party.

Suddenly, something hit me. What if no one saw Professor Bradford at the party because he was wearing a mask?

Is Professor Bradford the wolf in Evelyn's dream?

"This is good information, Evelyn. What do we do now?"

Evelyn crossed her arms as she pondered my question. "That depends on which way I decide to go. If I want my gift to go away, I do nothing and go back to bed. The only way for me to rid myself of my gift is to stop following the clues."

We had come so far to figure out the Aurora connection. If Evelyn stopped now, we may never solve Sloane's disappearance. But if Evelyn wanted to play it safe, then I would respect her decision to walk away from her gift.

"Tell me what you're thinking, Leo. This is what you want, right?" Evelyn wrung her hands nervously and stared at the sketchbook and pencils on the coffee table, eager to grab her art supplies and get to work.

Everything became clear at that moment. Evelyn never wanted to stop using her gift—she was only doing it because she wanted to please me. I'd crushed her spirit when I accused her of lying, and her solution was to become a different person to save our relationship.

"I'm going to ask you something point blank, Evelyn. All I want is the truth."

Evelyn nodded.

"What do you want to do about your gift? Forget about me. If nothing was standing in your way, what would you do right now?"

Evelyn's jaw tensed as she considered my question. "What matters now is us. I can't keep doing things that put us in danger—"

"Answer my question, Evelyn."

She stared out the window where her dream had taken place. Her big blue eyes shined as the early morning rays of sunshine warmed her pale skin.

"I would draw for the dead. I would find out what Sloane was trying to tell me, and I would do everything in my power to help her find peace."

Damn right, Evelyn.

I was a selfish jerk for wanting my alluring and wickedly talented girlfriend to change a single thing about her. All the things my friends and family had sworn to me I loved about Evelyn all got validated at that moment.

I knew why I had fallen in love with her—we shared the same values about helping people and would stick our necks out to serve the living—and, apparently, the dead.

"What do you need to get started? A pencil and paper?"

Evelyn smiled when she realized we were back on the same team. "I'll get my sketchbook and art supplies. Thank you, Leo." Evelyn gave me a quick hug, then ran off to gather the goods.

She set up a blanket on the floor and lit all the candles in the room. "I may draw for a few minutes or a few hours. No matter what happens, don't wake me until my hand stops moving. Questions?"

I backed away and gave Evelyn space to work. "How could I have ever doubted you?"

"You have a lifetime to make it up to me, Detective." Evelyn closed her eyes and held the tip of her pencil to the paper in the ready position.

Moments later, her hand moved across the page.

CONNECTED—LEO

*I*t was like a graphic murder unfolding before my eyes.

Watching Evelyn draw was the most miraculous and disturbing thing I had ever witnessed. The artist appeared to be in a trance as her hand moved across the paper and filled the pages of her sketchbook with eerie ghosts and spooky scenes.

As a homicide detective, I recognized the tiny details penciled into her sketches that law enforcement officers record at crime scenes. Blood splatter, stages of decay, footprints, signs of a struggle, broken glass…

As I watched Evelyn work, her hand partially obstructed my view. Hours later, Evelyn's hand stopped moving. When her work was complete, she lay down and fell asleep on the floor.

I tucked a pillow under her head and covered her with a blanket to make her comfortable while she rested. I lifted her sketchbook from her hand and examined her sketches.

Three drawings.

Three wickedly different scenes.

The first one was the creepiest of the lot. Evelyn had drawn the ghost of Aurora Livingston, clutching Sloane Matthews in her arms. Aurora's protective embrace portrayed her as a mother bear, willing to shred anyone who dared harm the young woman.

Does this mean Aurora and Sloane are together in the afterlife?

The next drawing was less ominous and more on the nose. It was a sketch of me holding a picnic basket. Nothing else. No background, even. In the Grimm fairytale, Red carried a basket with her to Grandmother's house.

Whatever it meant, it validated the theory that my assault was connected to the case. In the third drawing, Evelyn had sketched a shadowy figure lying on the ground in a crumbled heap—with an axe buried in the subject's back.

Through the darkness, a hundred sets of eyes glowed in the background, all fixated on the mangled body. Above the unidentified corpse, Aurora Livingston's ghost lurked in the background.

What the hell did Aurora Livingston, the creepy dolls, myself, and Sloane Matthews have in common?

WRONG—EVELYN

$\mathscr{A}$ gentle hand rubbed my back, waking me from a deep sleep.

I opened my eyes and found Leo crouched beside me on the floor. "How are you feeling, Evelyn?"

"I'm okay. What did I draw?"

"Catch your breath before we go over the drawings. You're in for a shock." Leo helped me to my feet, guided me into the kitchen, and poured a glass of water. According to him, I had sketched for hours and then crashed.

I checked the time. It was nearly five o'clock in the evening.

No wonder my energy is zapped.

Once I could focus, I asked Leo to show me the drawings. Yikes. Leo was right—my drawings told a very disturbing story. As I studied the sketches, we brainstormed about how Aurora and her dolls might be connected to the Sloane Matthews investigation.

We made a list of all the possible reasons, but we didn't have any evidence to support our theories.

"We need to bring Parker in on this," Leo said. "He knows more than we do about the details of the investigation."

"Agreed. I'm certain this place, or Aurora, holds the key to solving the case of Sloane Matthews, but—"

"But?" Leo asked.

"Where is Cora Bradford in all this? We know she's the one who called you the morning of the assault. The bartender thought it might be her with Nolan at the restaurant. So far, I haven't drawn her, nor has she appeared in my dreams. What are your thoughts on that, Detective?"

Leo gave me a smile, enjoying our collaboration. "Good point, partner. I'm not an expert in paranormal matters, but when it comes to murder—there is always a motive. If Cora had a hand in Sloane's disappearance, jealousy over the affair could've driven her to kill."

"Ghosts have a motive, too. There are three reasons why a restless spirit remains earthbound: fear, love, or revenge."

"Interesting." Leo pointed to the sketch of the slumped-over body. "Are your automatic drawings definitive? Have the events already taken place?"

"No. Sometimes I have premonitions—I see things that haven't happened yet but could happen in the future."

Leo stepped back for a moment, as if deep in thought. He turned his attention away from the drawings, picked up my hand, and led me outside. As we basked in the late afternoon sunshine, Leo stared into my eyes.

"This rarely happens to me, Evelyn, but I can't come up with the right words to describe what I'm feeling right now. In my life, I've never met anyone as interesting and talented and gorgeous and brave as you, but—"

Leo pecked me softly on the lips. "I've realized something about you. You're the kind of person who always wants to be right. Is that a safe assumption, Miss Sinclair?"

I cracked up at Leo's spot-on observation. "Well,

Detective, I have proven you wrong frequently over the last year. What specifically do you think I'm wrong about?"

"Last night. I told you I loved you. I meant it, Evelyn. I can see now what everyone has been trying to tell me all along—you are an amazing woman. I can't imagine living a single day without you."

Leo leaned in and kissed me passionately. His rough beard scratched my skin as we made out on the balmy fall day. I hugged him and snaked my hand up his shirt, scratching my long nails over his skin and kneading his muscular back.

"I love you, Leo. Forever."

"I love you, too. Thank you for giving me a second chance."

Our make-out session was about to lead us back to the bedroom, but the house phone rang, momentarily stealing my attention away from my sexy boyfriend. "Hold that thought, babe." I pulled myself away from Leo, ran back inside, and answered the phone.

"Hello?"

"Hi, Lauren. This is Angela. How is your stay?"

"Perfect. Everything is great. What can I do for you?"

"I have a special invitation for you from the horse barn. We are hosting a sunset run for experienced riders, and you have been hand-selected to join us."

"Horseback riding at sunset?" I said aloud for Leo's sake. "When does it start?"

"We're all saddled up. Your favorite horse, Bella, is ready for you. We can meet you at the bend in about fifteen minutes?"

"Fifteen minutes?"

"Go," Leo whispered. "I'll talk to Parker while you're gone."

"Yeah, sounds amazing. I'll meet you there. Thanks for thinking of me, Angela."

I hung up the phone. "Are you sure you don't mind, babe?"

Leo leaned in for a smooch. "This weekend is all about relaxing and having fun. Enjoy yourself. I'll be here when you get back."

I slid on my jeans, jumped into my boots, and wrapped a fall-themed skeleton scarf around my neck. As I headed out the door, I felt a rush of gratitude that Leo and I were headed on the path to rekindling our relationship.

The detective and I were back on the same team, and everything I wanted in life was coming into view. Now that Leo and I were together again, Vaughn's premonition would never come to pass.

My dream life with Leo begins now.

I was falling in love with Leo all over again.

As I crunched through the fall leaves on the way to meet my fellow riders, I felt energized and alive with a fresh sense of freedom.

The old Leo would've never allowed me to walk out the door alone, disappear into the woods without a cell phone, and ride off with a group of strangers. I had grown accustomed to Detective Ricci's rules about my safety.

When I had a new client, he ran a background check before giving me the okay to work with them. If I wanted to hang out with my friends, he had to know who I was going out with and precisely where we would be.

Even going for a walk required strict guidelines.

"Keep your phone in hand, always carry your personal protection device, and never talk to strangers or, God forbid, draw for the dead in public."

While these demands made Leo seem like a control freak, we had both learned the hard way that I could never be too careful in Chicago.

But I was safe at Livingston Farm. No one knew me here.

I had kept my identity a secret, and this was my chance to relax, hike through the woods without fear, and join a group of like-minded horse lovers on a dreamy sunset ride through paradise.

The spot where Angela said to meet the group was just around the bend. As I hiked the trail and inhaled the earthy scent of the season, I listened for hooves pounding on the dirt trail, voices, or any approaching sounds that would signal the group was near.

The woods were quiet, nothing but the wind rustling through the leaves, chirping birds, and crows cawing overhead. Hearing the birds reminded me I needed to call Vaughn and let him know I was all right.

Leo and I could call him together when I returned to the cabin. We owed him our sincerest gratitude for bringing us back together and leading us to Aurora—thanks to his new gift.

When I made it to the bend, I was surprised the group hadn't arrived yet. I was running about five minutes late, but I was certain they wouldn't have left me so quickly.

I rounded the corner and spotted a pickup truck with the Livingston Farm logo on the side parked on the main road at the bottom of the hill. Maybe Angela meant she would pick me up and then take me to the barn to join the others?

I was so excited about the invitation. Maybe I misunderstood her instructions. No matter. I headed down the hill to meet her on the road. The embankment was steep, and I had to be careful not to slip and twist my ankle.

When I reached the truck, I went to the passenger side window and peeked inside.

No one was there.

Thinking that maybe Angela had gone up the hill to track me down, I turned and—

Someone slammed me to the ground from behind and

wrapped a long leather horse lead around my body so swiftly that I didn't comprehend what was happening at first.

I struggled to breathe. As I tried to wrestle out of my attacker's stronghold, the sound of a woman laughing shook me to the core.

"Who are you? Why are you doing this?"

When the woman secured the strap, she pulled me to my feet and shoved me against the side of the truck. "You don't recognize me, Evelyn?"

My eyes widened in horror. "Angela? What are you doing? How do you know my real name?"

She tilted her head in mock pity. "Sadly, none of this is your fault. My husband is the one to blame." The way she said husband…it didn't sound right. This woman is unstable.

"Look—"

"No, you look." Her eyes were wide, and she was squeezing my arms so tightly it felt like she might crush my bones. My God, she was having some kind of psychotic break or something. "Finding Detective Ricci's girlfriend all alone out here was a pleasant surprise, too perfect to pass up."

She flashed a deviant smile. "Of all the places in the world you could've run, you ended up on my doorstep. Imagine my surprise when you checked into the Livingston Farm—the place I've been hiding since I knocked out Detective Ricci and fled Chicago."

Angela attacked Leo?

She shoved me into the backseat of the truck, then strapped me into the seat belt to keep me in place. A moment later, the driver's side door opened. My captor hopped inside. The engine revved. As she sped down the road, a million thoughts raced through my mind as the truth settled into my bones.

"You're Cora Bradford," I said. I'd seen pictures of her

when I researched Sloane's disappearance, but the woman in front of me now looked nothing like the mousy, brown-haired professor's wife who had been humiliated by her cheating husband's affair with his student.

My captor shot me that psychotic smile again. She pulled off her long auburn wig and tossed it on the passenger seat. Now that I knew for certain who she truly was, my blood ran cold as the images of Sloane's hacked-up body raced through my mind.

Is this what Cora plans to do to me?

Why had I let Evelyn walk alone?

While I updated Parker on Evelyn's new drawings, my gut was telling me I fucked up. "Correct. She had the dream and then sketched the new drawings right after."

We were out in the middle of nowhere. Anyone could be lurking in the woods, watching and waiting for the perfect opportunity to strike. I didn't want to be the one to bring it up, but after what Evelyn had gone through in the past, I was surprised she hadn't asked me to walk her to her meeting spot.

I was suspicious by nature, but I was certain I had taught Evelyn how to protect herself, and she would never just leave the house alone without a personal protection device and her—

Fucking hell. Evelyn's new phone was sitting on the kitchen counter.

When had I let my guard down and become so trusting? After my girlfriend had nearly died at the hands of a serial killer, it surprised me I let her leave the house without a bodyguard.

Next time, I'll be more careful.

"Right. Evelyn and I both agree there's a connection between Aurora Livingston and her dolls, the Sloane Matthews investigation, my attack, and Professor Bradford."

"Evelyn stayed in a room with the dolls?" Parker asked.

"Yeah, her first night here."

"I have an idea," Parker said. "Since there is no way to get a warrant based on Evelyn's drawings, why don't I check into the room? If there is something there, hiding in plain sight, I'll find it."

"Good point, Agent. But if it's as creepy as Evelyn says it is, you may have to sleep with the lights on."

Parker ended the call by saying he would be there in a few hours and would call once he had access to the room. I couldn't fathom how there could be a connection between an eighty-year-old ghost and her dolls, but Evelyn's gift was phenomenal, and I would never underestimate her talent again.

I took a quick shower and tried to convince myself not to worry about Evelyn. She was smart. We'd been together for a year. Surely I'd trained her to defend herself.

So why was my gut telling me she was in trouble?

As I got dressed, I decided to go down to the lodge and speak to that Angela lady and insist someone reach the group and confirm Evelyn had made it safely. Something I should've done from the start when I realized Evelyn had left her phone in the cabin.

I opened the bedroom door, stepped into the living room, and—

Click-click.

Someone cocked a gun behind my head.

"I'm not afraid to shoot you, Detective. Put your hands up and turn around slowly."

I was trained for situations like this. The number one rule in a crisis is to stay calm, assess the situation, and act accordingly. My first challenge was to avoid getting shot in the back of the head.

I lifted my hands and followed the gunman's directions. When I turned around and laid eyes on the shithead weasel who had gotten the jump on me—again—I wanted to drop him to the floor.

Of all the suspects I had encountered throughout my law enforcement career, this guy was the last person on this earth I would imagine had the balls to break into my cabin and press a gun to my head. Professor Nolan Bradford.

"Don't do anything stupid, Leo. Just—hear me out, okay?" Nolan's hand trembled, and the crazed look in his eyes alerted me he was riding high on a self-destructive path that made him a very dangerous man.

As I stared down the barrel of a pistol, I realized Evelyn was out in the woods somewhere, unprotected, while a suspected killer was hunting me down. What if he had found her first and forced her to tell him where I was?

At this moment, Evelyn could be injured, tied up, and locked in the trunk of his car, or worse. Nolan might have hurt her in other ways to satisfy his lust for young, beautiful women.

"Where the fuck is Evelyn?" The idea that this cowardly prick had touched my vulnerable girlfriend got my blood pumping with bad ideas. I had to restrain myself from lunging forward and tackling that gun-toting psychopath until the time was right.

"I don't know. I don't know what happened to Evelyn. She could...she might not be okay. She might've already done it. That's why I'm here. You need to listen to me. We need to find Evelyn before it's too late."

"What the fuck are you talking about, Nolan?"

"I know you think I killed Sloane—but I'm innocent. I can prove it, but I need you to come with me and stop the real killer. She's off the rails, and I'm afraid she's going to hurt Evelyn."

"Who?"

"Cora!" Nolan's eyes were wild with rage as he pinned his mistress's murder on his wife. "She found out about the affair and killed Sloane the night of the bonfire."

"Why didn't you tell me this when I interrogated you about her murder?"

"Sloane had given me an ultimatum—leave my wife, or it was over between us. She told me to make up my mind, and if I wanted to be with her, then I was to meet her at the party."

Nolan shook his head. "My marriage to Cora had been over for years, but she wouldn't sign the divorce papers. I wanted to be with Sloane, but I decided it was best for my student to end our relationship. I never went to the bonfire to meet Sloane."

The facts weren't adding up. "Your car was there that night."

"Cora swiped my cell and read the message from Sloane about the meeting. She took my car and went to the party to confront Sloane about the affair. I didn't know Cora killed Sloane until months later."

"What does this have to do with Evelyn?"

"Cora's pissed at you for not charging me with murder. She wanted to see me rot in prison, and when you failed to charge me, she set out to seek revenge on both of us. I'm afraid she's going to kill Evelyn to get back at you and pin the murder on me to seek vengeance."

Sweat dripped down Nolan's face as he revealed his wife's plan to ruin his life. "She kept some of Sloane's remains. She wouldn't tell me where she hid them, but she planted my DNA with her remains."

"Why didn't you come forward with this information?" I asked.

"I tried, Detective. You really don't remember what happened at the park?"

"I know you were there. You had a brown paper bag and were about to hand it over to me. After that, I don't remember what happened."

"Right! Now you understand. I was trying to do the right thing, but Cora—look, we don't have time to waste. I'll explain everything when we get on the road."

"Put down the gun," I said. "I need to call for backup."

"No. I can't do that, Detective. I have to finish this." He aimed the weapon between my eyes. "I'm going after Cora with or without your help. Are you with me?"

"Help me find Evelyn. If Cora is guilty, you have my word, she'll pay for her crimes."

Nolan tossed me a set of handcuffs. "Put these on. When we find Cora, I'll let you go. Deal?"

I snapped the bracelets on and tightened them. "Deal. Take me to Evelyn."

DEFLATED—EVELYN

If I had any hope of surviving my ordeal, I needed to free myself from these restraints.

Since I doubted Angela—Cora—would kill me while driving, I had time to plan my escape. Wherever she was taking me, I had to be ready to fight the moment my kidnapper opened the door.

Just like Leo had taught me.

Once I had a plan, I tried to figure out why Cora had come after me. My mental energy wasn't sharp enough to put all the pieces together, not after hours of automatic sketching, but the most logical motive I could think of was that Cora had killed Sloane and was trying to frame her husband for murder.

Now Leo and I were a part of this Lover's Revenge game.

Cora was driving down what I assumed was a back road on the Livingston property. The farmland spanned for miles, and I reasoned she was taking me somewhere off the beaten path so she could execute her devious plan—which was still a mystery to me.

It may be an hour or more before Leo realizes something

is wrong. I may not have that much time left. I had to stop Cora before we made it to Location B. Allowing her to control the situation was a losing game plan.

I had to strike first. A beautiful fall sunset lit up the sky, signaling a shift change in the natural world. It would be dark soon, and I could use the cover of night to hide from my captor. All I had to do was come up with a plan to escape and ride out the night, hiding in the darkness.

As I tested the security of the leather straps, someone hissed my name. Then a cold, dead hand touched my shoulder.

"Evelyn."

Cora and I were the only two people in this vehicle. I whipped my head around to see who was with me. I gasped when I spotted a ghostly form beside me—Sloane Matthews.

"Stop the truck, Cora. Let me out." I rarely saw ghosts outside my dreams, and I feared this was an ominous sign that I would soon join Sloane in the afterlife.

"What's the matter with you?" Cora checked over her shoulder to see what I was freaking out about, but as soon as she did, Sloane disappeared.

When Cora turned back around, the ghost was standing in the middle of the road. Cora's eyes widened in shock at the sight of Sloane's hacked-up corpse.

She can see the ghost, too.

Cora yanked the steering wheel sharply to the left to avoid a collision. Then she yanked it the right, over-correcting her mistake.

As the tires squealed, I closed my eyes and braced for impact. Instead of slamming into a tree, the truck veered off the road and slid down the embankment.

The tinny sound of metal being crushed on impact mixed with our screams as the truck crash-landed at the bottom of the ravine.

Cora groaned as she pushed away the deflated airbag. My stomach ached, and my chest was tight from the force of the seat belt that likely saved my life. I was so disoriented from the crash that I couldn't tell if the truck had landed upside down or right side up.

All that mattered was that Sloane Matthews had given me an opportunity to escape.

Run, Evelyn!

LOVELESS—LEO

"*D*rive." Nolan aimed the gun at me and motioned to the driver's side of his car.

I was handcuffed, but Nolan must've figured out I would strike if he let his guard down behind the wheel.

He was right.

"I think I know where Cora is taking Evelyn," Nolan said. "The Farm has an equipment storage facility at the edge of the property. It's private, and no one will be there after hours."

The fact that Nolan was leading me to Evelyn gave me hope that there was still time to save her. As I raced down a desolate country road, the quaint country houses flew by in a blur, and all I could think about was Evelyn.

"Slow down. You're going to kill us both," Nolan said.

I ignored him and kept the pace of a racecar driver heading into the last lap. As I focused on the road ahead and came up with a plan of attack, I was momentarily distracted by a crunching sound. Nolan was eating an energy bar.

"My body requires fuel. I need all the energy I can muster to take down Cora. When did you eat last, Detective?"

My job was to protect and serve, but at this moment, when Evelyn's life was on the line, I had never wanted to beat the crap out of someone more in my entire life.

My adrenaline rush will get me through this, jackass.

Sparring with Nolan wouldn't help me reach Evelyn, so I canned my smartass retort and focused on my job of saving the woman I love. What I needed now was information. I didn't want to go into my rescue mission without knowing what I was up against.

"How did Cora kill Sloane?"

"With an axe." Nolan's expression flushed with sadness. "I know you think I'm guilty of the crime, but I adored Sloane. She was sweet and kind and didn't deserve what happened to her. Cora murdered her out of jealousy."

"How do you know Cora killed her with an axe?"

"Cora wanted me to suffer for my betrayal. She killed Sloane, dismembered her body, and burned her remains in the bonfire. No one had reported Sloane missing, so by the time the crime was reported, Cora had gone back to the scene, collected her bones, and kept them to blackmail me into staying with her."

"Why are you telling me this now? You had plenty of chances to report the crime when I interrogated you."

"First of all, I didn't know Sloane was dead. I thought she was upset after our breakup and went away for a few days. Once Sloane was out of the picture, Cora tried to repair our loveless marriage. When I refused her advances, she confessed to the crime and threatened to plant evidence and pin the murder on me if I tried to leave her."

Nolan's jaw tensed. "Second, I did contact you, Detective. I used a recording of Cora's voice to get you to agree to meet me at the park. I knew you would never agree to meet me alone. All I wanted was to come clean and tell you everything, but Cora found out what I was up to and knocked you out before I could hand over the evidence."

Finally, the scene at the park came full circle. I remembered seeing Nolan there, but someone else had hit me from behind. "You're telling me Cora attacked me at the park? She killed Sloane and was trying to prevent you from turning her in?"

"Cora has to pay for her crimes against Sloane, me, and even you, Leo. Desperate times call for desperate measures. This was not how I wanted this to end, but since you and everyone else in the city believe I'm guilty, I have to prove Cora is the killer."

THIS WAS A TWISTED, fatal attraction, but all I cared about at the moment was Evelyn.

As I sped toward the location, I noticed a set of skid marks on the road. I pulled the car over. Nolan and I got out and rushed to the median.

There was a vehicle at the bottom of the ravine.

"That's Cora's truck."

Without fearing the consequences, I ran down the hill to check for survivors.

SINISTER—EVELYN

J lifted my head to reorient myself after the crash.

My body ached, and I was disoriented, but otherwise, I had no severe injuries. Luckily, Cora had buckled me into my seatbelt to keep me still in the backseat. I struggled in my restraints and clicked the release button.

As I attempted to escape through the back, the door flew open, and a set of strong hands yanked me out of the truck. The second my feet hit the ground, I drew my leg back and rammed my knee between Cora's legs.

Leo had taught me how to defend myself against a man, but when Cora groaned in agony and cursed my name, I was proud of myself for sticking to my training and fighting for my survival. While she was down, I rushed toward the tree line.

My legs were wobbly, but I forced myself to keep going. Without looking back, I headed for cover in the denser part of the woods. Just as I reached the fork in the road, my body lifted into the air and landed on the ground with a loud thump!

The force of the impact knocked the wind out of me. As I lay there, trying to catch my breath, Cora hovered over me with the leather straps in hand. "Don't fight me, Evelyn. You're only making this harder for yourself. I want you in perfect condition for Nolan."

"Let me go. You'll never get away with this."

Cora pulled me along by the leather horse leads and steered me toward an old Victorian house set way back in the middle of the woods. As we approached the remote home, I read the wooden placard posted in front of the white picket fence.

"Welcome to the Doll House. Home of Aurora Livingston 1901-1942."

Holy crap. This is the setting of my recurring nightmares —the place where Sloane has been leading me since the night of Leo's attack. What baffled me was why the ghost wanted me to come here.

What connection did Sloane have to Aurora? The women died decades apart, but they seemed united in death. Had Sloane been kidnapped from the party and killed way out here in another state?

Was her body buried in a shallow grave on the property? Are the ghosts connected by location, or was it possible the women were blood-related?

Whether I wanted to know the truth or not, Cora Bradford was dragging me into that house. Soon, I would find out what she and her husband Nolan were up to and why they had brought me and Leo into their sinister game.

Where are you, Leo?

Cora wrestled me into the house and then dragged me up a flight of stairs.

Fight, Evelyn. Don't let them win.

I used my body weight and slammed against her, sending

us both tumbling backward down the stairs. My head banged on the ground. My vision blurred, and then everything went dark.

UNHOLY—EVELYN

The putrid scent of firewood and death pulled me out of a deep sleep.

I opened my eyes and found myself in a darkened room surrounded by an army of vintage dolls. They were scattered all over the floor as if the precious dolls had been discarded like trash. Their small bodies lay tangled, and some had deep cracks in their delicate little skulls—like my dream.

Why had someone damaged Aurora's prized possessions? I gasped at the sight of all the lifeless eyes staring at me as I sat tied to a chair with leather leads inside the creepy old house.

I had a vague recollection of Cora wrestling me up the stairs, shoving pills into my mouth, and her taunting words. "These will make you sleepy, Evelyn. When you wake up, Nolan will be here."

My head was throbbing from the drugs, and the heavy scent of fresh flowers filled the room. I nearly gagged when I realized Cora had dressed me in Sloane's ill-fated Little Red Riding Hood costume—the same dress she wore when she appeared to me in my dreams.

If Cora had possession of this dress, that meant she had taken it off her corpse. I winced at the white lace-up corset that accentuated my bosom and the dainty red bows that trailed down the sexy, yet sweet, costume.

The blue and white skirt had been freshly pressed, and the fairytale character's infamous red cloak carried the scent of sweet perfume. Acid came up my throat when it became clear Cora had dressed me up to make me more desirable for Nolan.

The husband and wife are working as a team.

I struggled against my restraints and was prepared to gnaw off the leather straps if it meant I could free myself and tear off this costume. As I tried to escape, footsteps tapped up the stairs.

A moment later, Cora entered the room and approached me with that wicked smile. The psycho was wearing a long vintage nightgown and was holding a wicker basket in one hand and a bouquet of freshly picked flowers in the other.

I realized this whole messed-up game was some fairytale cosplay that had ended in murder. The kinky professor and his nutty wife were playing out a fantasy that led to the death of an innocent college girl—and I'm next.

"What is wrong with you, Cora? Why are you doing this?"

Cora dropped flower petals around the chair where I was tied up. "You look lovely, Red. Better watch out—the Big Bad Wolf will be here soon."

Sickened by the thought of what was about to go down, I searched the room in search of a weapon or anything I could get my hands on to defend myself against Cora.

Aside from the dolls, there was an old chest, but nothing else. As I processed the scene, I noticed something was missing...where is the axe?

I scanned the room, knowing the weapon had to be somewhere close by. The murder weapon had appeared in my dreams and in my drawings, and if the fucked-up Bradfords were playing out a sick fantasy, they would undoubtedly bring it into their role-playing.

As I recalled the Grimm fairytale, I remembered there were four characters. Red, Grandma, the wolf, and the huntsman. If I was Red and Cora was Grandma, what role was Nolan playing? The antagonist or the hero?

"I'll do whatever it takes to satisfy my husband's fantasies, Evelyn." Cora fingered the dainty red bow on the center of the corset, then trailed her hand down the curve of my silhouette.

"Nolan craves the flesh of young, beautiful women. Who am I to deny my husband's carnal needs? He can have your body, Evelyn. But he will always belong to me."

"You're insane, Cora," I said. "You'll never get away with this."

"Don't be frightened, Little Red." Cora stared into my eyes and caressed my cheek. "The pain won't last long. Give in to Nolan's demands, and he will reward you in ways beyond your wildest imagination."

Suddenly, a door burst open on the main floor.

"He's back." Cora smiled and untied me from the chair, then led me downstairs.

When we entered the living room, Professor Bradford stepped into the house, leading his prisoner—Leo.

Seeing him held at gunpoint by a suspected killer gave me the sinking feeling that we would not live to see the sunrise. Once again, my gift had gotten us into a situation we may not survive.

"My darling, Nolan!" Cora beamed. "You brought me a surprise."

"As promised." Professor Bradford bowed gallantly. "All our dreams will come true tonight, my dear. No more running. No more hiding. Once we destroy the evidence and silence the witnesses, we will free ourselves from the investigation. Then nothing will stop us from being together."

Leo's eyes filled with rage as Cora strapped me to a chair with leather restraints. As a couple, we had survived hellish circumstances and beaten the odds when faced with life-threatening dangers.

But this was different.

The Bradfords weren't just evil. They were insane. Now that they considered Leo—and now me—witnesses to the crime, they had nothing to lose by killing us to protect their dirty secrets.

If Leo and I had any hope of surviving the night, we had to figure out how to defeat a couple of delusional cosplayers at their own game. Nolan aimed the gun at the empty chair beside me and ordered Leo to have a seat.

Leo took one step toward the chair—

Wham!

He rammed his big body into Nolan so hard the professor stumbled to the floor, causing him to drop the gun. Leo chased the weapon as it skidded across the room, but Cora got to it first and aimed the weapon at Leo's chest. Her eyes were wild with rage, and I feared she was going to pull the trigger.

"Cora, no!" Nolan pleaded as he lumbered back to his feet. "Not yet. He's still useful to us. We need him to tell us what evidence he has against us." He softened his tone to reassure his wife. "Give me the gun."

"No," she said. "You're too weak to pull the trigger. I'll do the job when the time comes."

Cora ordered Leo to sit in the chair and said she would shoot me if Leo tried another stunt like that again. Once we were both helpless to strike against them, Nolan praised his wife for all her hard work.

"Now, tell me where you've hidden the bones," Nolan

said. "Once we collect all the evidence and tie up any loose ends, then we will silence the victims."

No way. I would not let Cora tear Leo and me apart. She was a vile human being, and I was prepared to drag the devil up from hell to stop her from harming the man I loved.

As I processed the Bradford's evil plan, the walls of the house began to close in on me. The living room was packed with Aurora's dolls and sentimental trinkets from the early 1900s. There were mechanical monkeys with tambourines, old-fashioned toys, a vintage record player, and century-old dusty artifacts.

After our murders, would Leo and I remain earthbound to seek revenge on our killers? Would we join the ghosts already here, lurking in the shadows of this old haunted house?

Keep it together, Evelyn. Leo needs you. Protect him at all costs.

Out of time and options, I summoned the only being who had a shot of taking down Cora.

"Sloane!" I unleashed a blood-curdling cry and summoned the ghost. She had come to me for help, haunted my dreams, and had the power to force Cora to crash her truck.

The feisty college student was hellbent on seeking revenge, and now she had a golden opportunity to do something about it now.

The room fell eerily silent. The temperature in the house dropped by twenty degrees. The windows rattled, and the dolls shook from a powerful supernatural force of energy that radiated around the room.

Ring…ring…ring…

An antique phone rang.

Cora's lips curled into a sinister smile as she lowered her gun and moved into the living room to answer the call.

Ring…ring…ring…

She lifted the phone off the receiver and pressed it to her ear. She paused a moment and smiled in anticipation. "Hello?"

Her eyes widened with an unholy expression of satisfaction. "Well, Sloane. What are you doing upstairs? I killed you once, and I'll do whatever it takes to silence you forever. Come to me, my dear. The Big Bad Wolf is waiting for you, Red."

Cora hung up the phone and retrieved her wicker basket. She reached inside, pulled out a mask, and assumed her role as the Big Bad Wolf.

Holy crap—Cora is the wolf. She killed Sloane.

The room fell eerily quiet as we waited to find out what was next.

The grandfather clock chimed, signaling the change in the hour. The floorboards creaked in the hallway.

"Get the axe, Mr. Huntsman," Cora said to Nolan. "It's outside in the shed."

The lights flickered, and the dolls opened and closed their eyes. One by one, their heads turned toward Cora as a frigid blast of air whooshed through the room. The tambourine monkey banged his cymbals, and a wind-up toy car rolled off the shelf.

Footsteps tapped down the stairs.

And then I held my breath as the ghost of Sloane Matthews made her grand entrance.

SHADOWS—LEO

Something creepy was going on in the house—but I had no idea what it was.

Evelyn sure seemed spooked by something, and Cora Bradford's sanity was no longer in question—the professor's wife had tipped over into the raving lunatic range. But if Cora wanted to play pretend and answer a phone that wasn't even connected to the wall, it was fine by me.

Her imaginary phone call probably saved my life—along with Evelyn's perfectly timed shout-out to the dead.

While Cora was fixated on something coming down the stairs, we had the distraction we needed to make our escape. I tried to get Evelyn's attention, but she was staring at the staircase just like Cora.

Mission accomplished, Evelyn. This is our chance to escape.

While Nolan was out of the room and Cora was lost in her fantasy, I slid my foot across the floor, hooked Evelyn's chair, and pulled her close until I reached the leather straps that bound her.

The knots were pulled tight, but I needed to loosen them

enough for Evelyn to wrestle herself free. "Evelyn. I need some help here." I tapped her foot to grab her attention.

When she realized what was happening, she got to work. Once she had enough wiggle room to slip out of the restraints, she slowly slid to the floor and helped loosen the rope wrapped around my arms.

I checked out the window and spotted Nolan coming back from the shed. "Go, Evelyn. Run as far away from here as you can. Don't worry about me."

Evelyn kept working to free me as if she hadn't heard a word I said. "Evelyn, get out of here."

"Hang on, I'm almost there."

The back door opened, signaling Nolan had returned from his errand to fetch the axe and was now inside the house. A second later, the rope loosened enough for me to break free from my restraints.

My hands were still cuffed, but I could run with Evelyn and get her to safety.

Footsteps padded down the hallway. Nolan was coming.

Cora was preoccupied with her delusion, giving Evelyn and me a tiny window of opportunity to escape. Quietly, I led Evelyn to the door while Cora's back was turned. I twisted the knob and guided Evelyn onto the porch.

I went behind her, using my body as a shield in case Cora busted us trying to escape and fired her weapon.

Once we were outside, Nolan yelled to his wife. "They escaped! We need to stop them. They know our plan, Cora!"

Evelyn and I raced for the safety of the trees, but before we could hide in the darkness, shots fired, and a bullet whizzed past my ear. Another one struck a tree trunk a couple of feet away.

"Keep running, Evelyn. Don't stop. If anything happens to me—" I groaned when my upper arm burned as if someone had held a red-hot poker against my skin. The bullet only grazed the skin, but it slowed me down enough that I stumbled and dropped to my knees.

"Get behind a tree. Now!" I snapped.

Instead of following my order, Evelyn pulled me back to my feet. She held me in a vise grip and steered me into the safety of the woods.

"Evelyn! Leo! I'm coming for you. You won't escape. I'll have your bodies all burned up before anyone knows you're missing."

I pulled Evelyn into my arms and pressed her head to my chest. "Don't move. Don't make a sound."

We remained silent as Cora passed by us and waited for her to move a safe distance away before heading in the opposite direction. As we slipped through the shadows, bright lights from an ATV beamed ahead.

A male shadow carrying an axe darted in front of the headlights before jumping on the back of the four-wheeler.

The professor had joined the search party.

SPLIT—LEO

Our odds of escaping had dropped significantly now that the Bradfords had lights, weapons, and an ATV.

But Evelyn and I had something those two maniacs didn't have—each other.

I had years of training under my belt and would use my brain and experience to outsmart them. As for my girlfriend, she was brave like my fellow blue-bloods and had as much grit as an entire battalion of soldiers.

My plan to survive the night was simple—divide and conquer.

Cora was the more significant threat because she had a gun—and she was delusional. She had already shot me in the arm and wouldn't hesitate to open fire if she spotted us.

Nolan was the weaker link. He was a desperate man who had gone to extremes to save his own skin. He was smart, but not in a tactical sense. I would follow my instincts and survival training by using any force necessary to protect myself and the woman I loved.

Evelyn and I darted between the trees and headed in the direction of the horse barn. We were miles away from it, but at least we were moving in a direction that would lead us to a populated area where we could call for backup.

"How is your arm?" Evelyn whispered.

"Fine. Just a flesh wound."

Suddenly, bright lights illuminated the trees just behind us. Nolan and Cora were circling back and heading in our direction.

"You won't get away from us," Cora yelled. "We're coming for you, Evelyn and Leo!"

They weren't far behind. We needed to get to higher ground and take a path too thick with brush and trees for the vehicle to follow. Evelyn's muscles tensed when she realized the danger we faced.

"Do you trust me, Leo?"

"Of course, but—"

"Sloane!" Evelyn whispered. "We need your help. If you can hear me, I need you to distract Cora and lead her away from us."

"Evelyn, be quiet. They're close behind. I don't know what your plan is, but no ghost is going to save us."

The vehicle was getting closer.

Beams of light bounced around us.

I tugged Evelyn's arm and pulled her behind a large tree. I peeked around the trunk and noted that Cora was walking beside the ATV while Nolan was driving slowly beside her and watching for our silhouettes to appear in the lights.

The vehicle stopped.

They must've spotted us.

While I pressed up against Evelyn to act as a human shield, she winced and plugged her fingers into her ears as if she heard a loud noise.

"Turn around!" Cora yelled. "We missed her. She's back there!" Cora yelled.

"No. We've already searched back there. They have to be hiding—"

"Didn't you hear her?" Cora said.

"Hear who?"

"Evelyn screamed my name. That bitch is taunting me now. I'm going after her. She and her boyfriend must've split up in different directions. You find Leo, and I'll go back and get Evelyn."

As her footsteps crunched through the leaves, the lights from the ATV closed in on us. I didn't know what Cora thought she heard, but nobody screamed her name.

DEAD END—EVELYN

Thank you, Sloane.

Now that Cora was following the ghost's voice and going in the wrong direction, Leo and I had a chance to outsmart Nolan.

As the vehicle approached, there was no time to make a plan of attack. I trusted Leo would know what to do, and I would follow his lead when the time came.

As the vehicle crept closer, Nolan called out, "Come out, Detective Ricci. I'm not going to hurt you. I was only pretending to go along with Cora so I could get her to confess and clear my name. You can trust me. I'm on your side."

Leo remained still as the headlights shined on the tree we were hiding behind. If Nolan was telling the truth, we could escape on the ATV before Cora figured out she was following a ghost instead of me.

The vehicle inched past our hiding place, prompting Leo to guide us ever so slightly around the tree so we could remain unseen. The moment Nolan had his back to us, Leo sprang into action like a crouching tiger lunging for the kill.

With his hands still cuffed in front of him, Leo lept onto the vehicle and barreled into Nolan, knocking them both to the ground with a loud thud.

Nolan groaned from the force of the blow and went off on an indignant, self-centered rant. "What is wrong with you? I'm trying to help you!" Nolan whined. "Cora is the killer. We need her to tell you where Sloane's remains are, so I can clear my good name once and for all."

"Trust a guy who held me at gunpoint? I don't think so, you fucking prick."

I stood there, stunned, as the sounds of fists on flesh and grunts and groans echoed through the woods. "What do I do, Leo?"

"Get the axe!"

What the hell? Taking Nolan's weapon was the right thing to do, but for the love of all things holy—I would not take a swing at the guy.

I hopped onto the vehicle and grasped the murder weapon. It was heavier than I imagined, and the idea of using it to chop a body into pieces sickened me. It was dark, but I could see two men fighting in the glow of the headlights.

From my vantage point, I watched Leo and Nolan circling each other like a pair of territorial street dogs. Leo was much bigger than Nolan, but was at a disadvantage because his wrists were cuffed.

Plus, Nolan had picked up a large stick and was aiming it at Leo's head. I had to intervene and up the odds in our favor. Since slicing Nolan with an axe was not an option, I searched the vehicle for another weapon.

I found a large metal Thermos in the cupholder—perfect.

As Leo ducked and weaved Nolan's charge, I hid behind the vehicle and waited for my moment to strike.

Leo issued a counterstrike with a swift kick to Nolan's upper thigh. The professor groaned, then retaliated by punching Leo square in the jaw. The force of the blow caused Leo to stumble.

The professor lifted the stick and aimed it at Leo's skull.

Act now, Evelyn. Leo needs you!

I sprang out from behind the ATV and whacked Nolan on the head with the heavy Thermos.

Nolan cried out in pain, but he was still on his feet.

I wasn't a violent person and obviously didn't swing hard enough to knock him out. As I held my position, panting, Nolan set his sights on me. His gaze took a lap around my body as I stood there in the Little Red costume holding the Thermos.

His lips curled into a wicked smile as a twisted fantasy played out in his mind. Nolan's obsession with fairytales and cosplay was evident in his lustful gaze. "You look good enough to eat, Evelyn."

He lunged forward, but before he could capture me, Leo pounced on his back and dropped him to the ground. Leo drove his knee into Nolan's back to render him helpless.

My take-charge boyfriend ordered me to remove my apron and use it to tie up Nolan. He was weak from being leveled by a brick wall of pure muscle, but he was still conscious and blabbering about his innocence.

"This is all Cora's fault. She killed Sloane. The evidence I tried to give you at the park was Cora's wolf mask. Believe me, I tried to do the right thing..."

"Hurry, Evelyn," Leo said. "We need to keep moving. Cora is still out there."

While I subdued the professor, Leo shoved a gag into his mouth. He killed the lights, clutched the axe, and scanned the woods for the killer. The air was still, and the nocturnal night shift was eerily quiet. The sound of nothingness was not normal—

"Bang! Bang! Bang!"

A gun went off. Bullets hit the ATV. I heard a loud pop when one of the back tires exploded, making the vehicle undrivable.

"Evelyn! Are you okay?" Leo grabbed my arm and dragged me around to the other side of the vehicle.

I eked out a yes as Leo and I commando crawled back to the woods. Without the vehicle, we had to make our escape on foot while dodging Cora's bullets.

"Keep running, lovebirds! The chase makes the game more exciting."

Leo guided us to higher ground. When we reached the top of the ridge, a barbed-wire fence enclosed the entire edge of the property. We had reached a dead end.

"Don't worry, Evelyn. I'll find another route."

As Leo took my hand and led us in another direction, an ominous, blue-tinted female figure appeared before me. The ghostly woman lifted her arm and pointed her long, bony finger at a lonely tree at the bottom of the ridge.

Moonlight shined in the clearing and illuminated a cluster of headstones—the Livingston family cemetery.

I stopped dead in my tracks.

This is the scene from my painting.

"Evelyn, what's wrong?" Leo asked.

"We're not alone."

"Who else is here?"

"Aurora."

DREAMS—EVELYN

"$\mathcal{D}$o you trust me, Leo?"

He hesitated a moment. "Evelyn, you need to let me take the lead. Cora's intention is to kill us. I'm trained for situations like this. One mistake could cost us our lives."

Leo's plan was to stay hidden in the woods and follow the creek back to the horse barn. In theory, that made sense. But every instinct in my body told me we were making a fatal mistake.

I came back to life with my gift for a reason. I had no explanation for why Aurora was pointing me toward her family's graveyard, why I dreamed of it, or why I had painted this same scene in my studio, but I believed it was a sign that would lead us to safety.

"We need to go there." I pointed to the old cemetery, visible under the moonlit sky. "Aurora is pointing the way. I know it's still hard for you to accept—"

"You want to follow advice from a ghost instead of me?" Leo scoffed.

"I've seen this place before in my dreams and in my art.

We'll be safe there. I can't tell you how I know, but I'm asking you to trust me, Leo."

A branch snapped.

We froze at the sound of impending danger.

Cora was closing in on us. Staying close to the fence was a death sentence. We had to move and put distance between us and the killer.

Accepting what I said, Leo squeezed my hand and led us toward the cemetery. I took the heavy axe from his hand, knowing Leo could not take a good hard swing while he was in handcuffs. When the time came, I would do whatever was necessary to save Leo and give us a fighting chance to live to see another day.

I finally had an answer to the question I had pondered earlier:

Who is the huntsman?

Me.

BLUNT—LEO

Trusting Evelyn might cost us our lives.

Cora was hot on our trail, and following the creek was the safest option. But also the most obvious. Our hunter had the advantage of knowing the land and thought she could trap us when we hiked the ridge and ran into the fence.

Evelyn's plan of hiding in plain sight was reckless—but was it so obviously wrong that it was actually right?

Evelyn carried the axe through the heavily wooded area. It would be difficult for me to use it while my hands were cuffed, so if it came down to a situation where we had to fight for our lives, I hoped Evelyn would find the courage to use the weapon against our attacker.

No decent human wanted to swing an axe at someone, but I wouldn't hesitate to save the woman I loved—and I hoped Evelyn would do the same for me.

When we reached the Livingston family graves, I told Evelyn to stay hidden behind a tree while I checked out our alleged safe haven.

Maybe I was a judgmental prick, but I didn't trust

Evelyn's ghost the way she did. I wasn't about to risk our lives and drag Evelyn into that creepy cemetery without running a recon mission.

"I'm going in first. If anything happens, follow the creek and get to the horse barn, understand?"

Evelyn patted my shoulder. "Thank you for trusting me. I know we'll be safe here."

I started with a visual sweep before stepping out into the open. I believed we'd lost Cora, but I wouldn't bet my life on it. There was a short iron gate that marked off the family plot.

I stepped over it, entered the cemetery, and walked the perimeter. There were no surprises here—just a cluster of graves under an old oak tree. I didn't need a paranormal gift or an elevated sixth sense to recognize that this place was more haunted than the nine levels of hell.

A frigid blast of air swirled around me when I stepped onto hallowed ground, and the hair raised on the back of my neck. Other than the fact that this place was unsettling, there was no reason we couldn't hide out here until Cora gave up her search and followed a different path.

I stepped back over the fence to get Evelyn—

"Freeze, Detective." Cora cackled with devilish delight as she aimed the gun at my chest. "I told you I would find you. Now tell me where your girlfriend is hiding."

A million thoughts raced through my mind. The most important one was how I was going to protect Evelyn. "We split up. I was slowing her down. She probably made it back to the farm by now and has already called for help."

"Lies. That little weakling would never leave her big, strong boyfriend." Cora cocked the gun. "Come out, Evelyn! I'll kill him right now if you don't show your face. One... two..."

"Stop!" Evelyn shrieked. "I'm coming out. Don't shoot him."

Cora flicked her eyes sideways, following the sound of Evelyn's voice.

While I was glad to have a reprieve from my execution, I thought it was strange Evelyn had traveled to the other side of the woods in such a short amount of time. Why had she left her safe spot in the first place?

Maybe her ghost had appeared again and led her in another direction.

Cora shifted her gaze between me and the woods where Evelyn called out to her. "Hurry up! I'm losing patience."

"Evelyn, no! Don't come out. Stick to the plan. Run!"

Cora's eyes were wild with homicidal rage as she aimed the gun at my chest. The only chance we had to stay alive was—

Whap!

Cora let out an animalistic scream, dropped the gun, and crumpled to the ground in a heap. A flicker of light flashed behind her as the moonlight reflected off the blade of the axe.

Evelyn stood behind Cora with the weapon held high, poised and ready to deliver another blow to my would-be killer. As I stared at the weapon, I noticed the blade was clean, which meant Evelyn had struck Cora with the blunt end of the wooden handle.

Evelyn's gentle soul wouldn't allow her to slice an axe into the killer's back like her premonition had foretold, but she was resourceful and did what she had to do to save my life. While Cora was out cold, I grabbed her gun.

Now that the threat had passed, Evelyn ran to me and wrapped me in her loving embrace. "I'm sorry I steered you wrong, Leo. You trusted me, and Cora nearly killed you."

I exhaled a sigh of relief as I held Evelyn in my arms.

"Maybe your ghost was right, Evelyn. We're alive. Our mission was to survive the night. Thanks to you—and your ghosts—we're the last ones standing."

Moonlight shined down as Evelyn stared into my eyes. "Does this mean you trust me now, Detective?"

"With my life, Evelyn."

HEAVENLY—EVELYN

*L*eo and I rested under the tree in the cemetery before making the long trek back to the farm.

Some people feared the darkness, but I embraced the elemental energy of the night. Leo leaned back against the mighty oak, and I rested my head on his chest. Feeling his heartbeat filled me with gratitude that we had survived.

As I thought about our future together and where Leo and I would go from here, a wondrous bright light swirled in the sky, and a tunnel opened in the heavens. As I stared into the blinding white light, I found myself inside Aurora's home.

At the top of the stairs, a beautiful woman in a vintage gown summoned me to follow her upstairs. She guided me into a bedroom and waved her arm at an antique hope chest basking in a warm golden light.

I moved closer and read a brass plate engraved with the name Aurora.

The angelic woman smiled and pressed her hand over her chest, as if introducing herself for the first time. The new, angelic Aurora waved her hand, and the top of the chest opened.

A radiant purple light swirled around the room, and the spirit of Sloane Matthews lifted out of the chest. The ghost's once morbid blue skin and life-ending gashes on her neck had disappeared.

Aurora's hope chest—that's where Cora had hidden Sloane's remains.

The mystery of how the women were connected was now solved. Now that Sloane's killer had been caught, it was time for her spirit to move on.

Sloane radiated a warm and colorful aura of pure love, peace, and joy. A chorus of angels sang an ancient melody as her spirit lifted into the heavens.

As her soul entered the tunnel and disappeared from sight, a family of beautiful children waved at Aurora and beckoned her to their eternal home. "Mama! Mama! Mama!"

The sweet sound of the children's voices filled the room as Aurora stared in wonder. She had waited almost a century for her dreams of motherhood to be fulfilled. She reached out to her precious children and embraced them as colors more beautiful than the world has ever known radiated around their heavenly bodies.

As Aurora's soul lifted, her gaze dropped back to the room. A hundred sets of doll eyes fixated on the woman who cared for them in life. Aurora reached down, picked up one of her dolls, and handed it to me for safekeeping.

Aurora's love for her earthly treasures carried over into the afterlife.

The Livingston children followed their mother's lead. They picked up each of the dolls and piled them before me as if charging me with their care. Once I understood my task, I placed my hand over my heart and gave the family a nod of acceptance.

Then Aurora and her children held hands and ascended into the heavens. The miracle of life had come full circle for Sloane and Aurora.

As the heavenly music faded and the tunnel closed, the sound of a dog barking snapped me back to the here and now. I was back at the cemetery with Leo, sitting under the tree.

"Do you hear that?" Leo asked.

"The dogs? Where are they coming from?"

"You'll see." Leo grinned as he helped me to my feet and led me out of the cemetery. The sun was peeking over the horizon, and a rooster sounded to kick off the start of a new day.

As the barking got louder, I finally realized what Leo had already figured out.

"Is that a search party? The dogs are looking for us?" As soon as I spoke the words, a yellow lab dragged his handler down the hill and barked wildly with excitement. I stared in disbelief as my sweet boy Duke led his handler to his target— us.

"Duke!" I dropped to the ground as the best boy in the world licked my face and wagged his tail as he completed another successful mission. Retirement never suited him anyway. Duke's handler, Officer Campbell, embraced her good pal, Leo, obviously relieved to find us safe.

"You're never going to let me live this down, are you, Campbell?" Leo asked.

"Hey, I can't let anything happen to Duke's favorite babysitter. I'd say we're even."

The rest of the search party gathered around us. The team apprehended our woozy abductor and read Cora her rights, while a fellow officer freed Leo from his handcuffs and called for a medic to treat Leo's gunshot wound.

"Evelyn!" Parker gave me a hug and breathed a sigh of relief to find us alive. "Help is on the way, Leo."

"I'm fine. It's just a flesh wound. I'm not going anywhere until I give you an update on what went down," Leo said. "Cora is the killer. She murdered Sloane out of jealousy."

"What about Nolan?" Parker asked. "Is he an accomplice?"

"No. He lured me to the park to hand over evidence to prove Cora was guilty. When she found out about his plan, she cracked me over the head to prevent her husband from ratting her out."

"Why didn't Nolan try to contact you again? If he had evidence, why not come clean?" Parker said.

"Cora was blackmailing him. She burned Sloane's body but kept her remains and threatened to pin the murder on him if he left her."

"That makes sense. We got a positive ID on the remains from the bonfire—they belong to Sloane Matthews."

Leo nodded, relieved they now had evidence of murder to take to the district attorney. "Did you find Nolan where we left him?"

"We did. He's got quite a story to tell," Parker said.

"Oh, I know. He abducted me at gunpoint from the cabin, kidnapped me, and held a Chicago P.D. detective, and a civilian, hostage. He won't escape a lengthy prison sentence, no matter how he spins his tale."

"Agreed. Cora's not talking, though, and Nolan claims he doesn't know where to find Sloane's remains."

"You'll find her bones upstairs," I told him. "Cora hid them in Aurora's hope chest."

"That was the connection between the women?" Leo asked.

I gave him a nod, then whispered, "Aurora and Sloane are free now. Mission accomplished. Their souls are now basking in eternal glory." I lifted my fist and gave my partners in crime, Leo and Parker, a celebratory fist bump.

"By the way, how did you know we needed help, Parker?"

"Something interesting happened. I got a call from Dr. Vaughn. He asked me if the word Duke meant anything to me." Parker gave me a knowing grin. "Thank God the three of you stayed in touch."

Way to go, Dr. Vaughn.

SPARK—EVELYN

"Where are you taking me, Leo?"

"If I tell you, then it won't be a surprise." The detective shot me an ornery grin as he drove through the suburbs toward a secret location.

Leo's memory still hadn't returned, but now that we were home, our relationship was as strong as ever. I even felt a fresh spark of attraction toward my new Leo. He was still the strong and brave hero I fell in love with, and it was like I got an added bonus of a new side of him I had never known.

Leo handed me a blindfold. "Put this on."

"Really?" My heart pounded with excitement as I followed my sexy boyfriend's command.

The car stopped. Leo turned off the ignition. A moment later, he opened my door, wrapped his arm around my shoulder, and guided me to my surprise.

When we reached the destination, Leo opened a door and led me inside. He removed my blindfold, kissed me on the cheek, and whispered, "Surprise."

I opened my eyes and found myself in an empty house. There was a gorgeous bouquet of wildflowers on the kitchen bar, along with a note with my name scrolled across the center. Leo motioned for me to open the card.

Dear Evelyn,

My life changed forever when I met the most amazing woman in the world. While our memories of the first encounter may be different, one thing remains the same. The chain that binds us will never break.

I love you more now than I ever dreamed possible. Here's to the first day of our new life together. Welcome home, beautiful.

Love, Leo

I wiped away my tears and turned to hug my sweet and loving boyfriend, but he was no longer beside me—Leo was down on one knee.

My heart swelled with joy as the love of my life presented a velvet box with a sparkling diamond engagement ring.

"Evelyn, since you came into my life, all my thoughts have revolved around you. At first, you were a beautiful stranger. An interesting and sexy woman I had the good fortune to share a bed with."

Leo took my hand and stared into my eyes. "I can't imagine living a single day without you, and never want to feel the pain of being apart again. I love you with all my heart. Will you marry me, Evelyn Sinclair?"

As Leo slid the ring on my finger, my heart warmed with gratitude. All the heartache and fear we'd experienced melted away, making room for new memories, along with the added bonus of becoming the future Mrs. Evelyn Ricci.

Everything we'd fought for and all the stress and heartache we endured was worth it. Leo and I were soulmates, and nothing in this world, or beyond, would ever tear us apart. "Yes, Leo. I'll marry you."

FLIPPED—LEO

"Hey, Ricci! Make mine medium-rare." Santoni lifted his PBR in salute as he called out his order.

Parker and I manned the grill while Mom and Evelyn set out the sides and salads for our first official Ricci Family cookout. Evelyn and I finished remodeling and moved into our new home shortly after we survived our ordeal.

On top of working with the Livingston Farm to register Aurora's home on the Indiana Historical Registry—and ensuring the antique dolls would remain with the house indefinitely—Evelyn and I had been incredibly busy.

I got cleared to go back to work and suffered no long-term effects from my head injury—except the fact that I lost a year's worth of memories. Instead of dwelling on the past, I looked forward to my future with Evelyn and resuming my position on the Violent Crimes Task Force.

We hadn't set a date for the wedding yet, but Evelyn and my sisters had been talking nonstop about flowers, string lights, and dresses, and made all sorts of plans for the bachelorette party and bridal shower.

I would get married in a cardboard box as long as Evelyn was in there with me. But for her, all the small details mattered. If my fiancée wanted floating orchid candles, pink champagne, and black lace bridesmaid gowns, who was I to deny my cool and edgy bride from having the wedding of her dreams?

As I flipped burgers and watched my nieces and nephews playing in the yard, listened to my friends swapping stories, Duke playing fetch, and my beautiful bride-to-be basking in domestic glory in our new backyard, I thanked the heavens for giving me a second chance at life and love.

It turned out that the last star on Evelyn's map led us back to Chicago—to our current address—another validation that Evelyn and I were destined to be together.

After the last of our guests left the party, my fiancée and I went to the kitchen to tidy up. She loaded the dishwasher, while I covered up the leftovers and placed them in the fridge.

As we worked, I stole glances at my sexy bride-to-be. She had on tight jeans and a sheer blouse, and I'd been admiring her body all day. Now that we were alone, I could do something about all the fantasies that had been running through my mind during the party.

I stopped and stared at Evelyn as she dried the last of the casserole dishes. When she busted me checking her out, her cheeks warmed with embarrassment. "See something you like, babe?"

Instead of answering, I prowled toward her like a hungry beast, stalking his sexual prey. Evelyn loved it when I took control and dominated her. She craved my strength, and I was more than happy to give her what she wanted.

"Leo, stop. What are you doing?" She swished the dish-towel at me and laughed as she moved around the counter to escape.

As I closed in on her, Evelyn locked her gaze on mine and backed up toward the living room. She unbuttoned her winter white blouse, enticing me to pursue her. When I got within snatching range, Evelyn giggled as she turned to run away.

I captured her from behind and wrapped my arms around her waist. I nibbled on her neck as I steered her into the living room and held her prisoner against the couch.

"Get ready for a hard and fast ride, beautiful." I unbuckled her leather belt, unfastened her jeans, and pulled them down her thighs and removed them. I slid my finger inside her lacy panties.

She moaned with satisfaction as I massaged her warm and wet femininity. "God, Leo. What are you doing to me?" When she came undone from my touch, I pulled down her G-string and bent her over the soft arm of the couch.

I parted her legs, saddled up behind her, and eased into her V. Evelyn gasped as my rock-hard erection thrust inside her while she held the cushions to steady herself. While I had her in that vulnerable position, I had complete control over my gorgeous prey.

The sensation of being so deep excited me, and I knew I wouldn't last long in this position. As promised, I gave it to her hard and fast. Sexy moans and the sounds of passion echoed through the room as our pleasure escalated.

As we climaxed together, Evelyn moaned my name as I savored my orgasm. After our quickie in the living room, it was official. Evelyn and I had christened every room in the house with our wild and exciting romantic encounters.

That evening, we snuggled under the blankets and listened to soft music as we settled in for the night. The weather had turned chilly since we moved in, and the trees had shed all their fall leaves.

With Evelyn resting on my chest, I closed my eyes and rubbed her back gently as we drifted off to sleep.

WHEN I OPENED MY EYES, Evelyn was already up, sketching beside the window. Her engagement ring sparkled in the light, and the morning sunshine warmed her face, giving her skin a healthy glow.

As I admired my beautiful fiancée—a year's worth of memories rushed back to my mind.

The day we met at the coffee shop, riding in the ambulance after she was attacked, hanging out at Mom's house, black tie parties, art shows, Evelyn wearing my old Loyola t-shirt…

Evelyn glanced up from her work when she realized I was awake. "Good morning, babe."

I blinked as I processed what was happening. "The first time we met at the coffee shop, you tore up the sketch you drew of me into a million pieces. Then you dumped the trash into my green smoothie cup."

I laughed at the memory. "You thought I was angry at you, so you lied when I asked you if you were a professional artist."

Evelyn flipped her sketchbook face down on the table and hopped into bed beside me. "Babe, what's happening? You remember the coffee shop? That memory was from the day we met. What else?"

I rambled on about our intimate date nights, pizza and beer with friends, baseball games, gallery events, our romantic beach vacation, sexy time in the bedroom with Evelyn in handcuffs, the minor kitchen fire caused by Evelyn's failed attempt at baking…

"Oh, Leo! Your memories are back!"

We laughed and reminisced about all the things I had

forgotten. Now that I remembered the first time we fell in love, it was like lightning striking for a second time.

Evelyn's joyful expression faded as she picked up her sketchbook and shot me a worried look.

"What is it? What did you draw? Did you have a premonition?"

Evelyn forced a smile and nodded. "I did, but I don't want you to freak out. It's a good thing—I think."

"Are you pregnant? Did you draw a baby?"

"No, Leo. We're not having a baby—but there's a big change coming for both of us." Evelyn turned the sketchbook over and showed me her drawing.

The picture was of us, but not in our current state. Evelyn had drawn me, flashing an agent's shield and wearing a baseball hat with the letters FBI embroidered on the cap.

In the same sketch, Evelyn had on a suit and held up her FBI employee credentials as well.

Evelyn and I are working for the FBI—together?

As I stared at the drawing, all I could do was shake my head in confusion.

"Does this mean what I think it means?" I asked.

"Looks like you're going to Quantico—Agent Ricci."

ABOUT THE AUTHOR

Kat Shehata is a New York Times bestselling author—with the help of a psychic.

After teaming up with world-renowned psychic Sylvia Browne, Kat co-wrote and published *Animals on the Other Side*, which became a New York Times bestseller.

Kat's writing career took a romantic turn when a story about a homicide detective and a woman who knows too much refused to let go. That story became the *Drawn to Death* series—gripping romantic suspense novels that blend murder investigations with high-stakes emotional tension.

Her work has earned two Benjamin Franklin Awards and the Killer Nashville Claymore Award for Best Suspense.

Kat holds a bachelor's degree in theatre from Wilmington College, a professional writing certificate from the University of Cincinnati, and an MFA in Writing from Spalding University. She splits her time between Cincinnati, Ohio, and Boca Raton, Florida, where she is always working on her next story.

ACKNOWLEDGMENTS

As with every book, there are many people to thank. The first round of book love goes to my incredibly supportive husband, Ash. The *Drawn to Death* world has become a part of our lives over the last few years, and we talk about the characters as if they are part of our family. I am blessed to have this wonderful man in my life.

Additionally, I want to send high-fives to my kids for always believing in me, reading my books, and cheering me on when I'm crushed by deadlines. Thank you to all my friends and family who support my career, and to my editor Deborah for helping my story reach its greatest potential.

Most of all, I want to thank you, dear readers! I have an artist's soul, and the most important part of my career is delivering books readers will love. Bloggers, reviewers, and readers, I appreciate your support more than words can express—group hugs to all the book lovers who support my writer's journey.